TROUBLE-MAKER

Andrew Clements

Illustrations by Mark Elliott

SCHOLASTIC INC.

ISBN 978-0-545-50507-9

Text copyright © 2011 by Andrew Clements.
Illustrations copyright © 2011 by Mark Elliott.
All rights reserved. Published by Scholastic Inc., 557 Broadway, New York, NY 10012, by arrangement with Atheneum Books for Young Readers, an imprint of Simon & Schuster Children's Publishing Division.
SCHOLASTIC and associated logos are trademarks and/or registered trademarks of Scholastic Inc.

12 11 10 9 8 7 6 5 4 3 2 1   13 14 15 16 17/0

Printed in the U.S.A.

This edition first printing, September 2012

The text for this book is set in Bembo.
The illustrations for this book are rendered in pencil.

For Robert Alexander Hanna,
one of my first friends
—A. C.

Acknowledgments

I want to acknowledge with deepest gratitude the fine work of all my friends and collaborators at Simon & Schuster and Atheneum Books for Young Readers, with a special thanks to my editor, Caitlyn Dlouhy.

TROUBLE-MAKER

CHAPTER ONE

NOT APPROPRIATE

Clay Hensley frowned at the paper on the table. It wasn't a very good drawing. He'd made tons of better ones . . . like that picture he'd made of the old man sitting on the bridge? Now, *that* was good—even won a prize. This drawing? It was okay, just a simple portrait. It wasn't going to win any prizes—but then, it wasn't supposed to. It was supposed to do something else. Soon.

Out of the corner of his eye Clay saw Mr. Dash get up from his desk. The class period was almost over, so the art teacher was beginning his inspections, same as always.

Clay squinted and kept working on the portrait, shading a little here, erasing a little there, trying to get the expression on the face just right—

actually, trying to get the whole head to look right. It wasn't easy.

Ears were hard to draw. The nose, too. And eyes? Forget about it. Not like drawing a tree. Or a piece of fruit.

Mr. Dash was at the back of the art room now, talking softly, moving from table to table.

"You see there, where the mountains meet the sky? Your lines need to be thinner and lighter there—it'll make everything seem farther away. Good detail work on that tree in the foreground."

Mr. Dash had to be talking to Marcia. She was the only kid in sixth grade good enough at drawing to get advice like that. Except for him.

Clay kept working on his drawing, but his hand was so tense he was squeezing the pencil. He picked up his eraser and made a correction . . . then he had an idea. He took his big brother's cell phone from the pocket of his jeans, carefully, so no one would notice—Mitch would *not* be happy if some teacher took it away from him. One-handed, he clicked to the camera function and took a photo of his drawing, then another. He slipped the phone back into his pocket and picked up his pencil again.

Mr. Dash was working his way along the tables in Clay's row now.

"Good improvement there, James."

The teacher shuffled a few steps closer.

"Those shadows? Don't push on your pencil—makes 'em look muddy."

"But I want them really dark."

That was BriAnne talking, two tables away.

"Then just use a pencil with softer lead—4B, or even 6B."

Clay pretended to be busy with his work, but he knew Mr. Dash was right behind him now, looking over his shoulder. He heard the teacher suck in a quick breath, and then hold it.

Clay began counting. One thousand one, one thousand two . . . The art teacher let his breath out slowly.

Then he spoke, his voice low and strained.

"Clay . . ."

Clay kept working.

"Clay, stop it. Stop drawing."

He turned around and looked up at Mr. Dash. "Why?"

"You know why, Clay. That's . . . not appropriate. Your drawing's not appropriate."

Clay put a confused look on his face. "You said we could draw *anything* today. And I wanted to draw a *jackass*."

4

Several kids laughed. The whole class tuned in, and the kids sitting close tried to get a look at his drawing.

Clay had a hard time not smiling. He was already imagining how fun it was going to be to tell his brother, Mitch, about this.

Mr. Dash raised his voice a little. "Please don't say 'jackass.'"

Clay rolled his eyes. "Fine. I wanted to draw a *donkey*. A stupid-looking donkey, that's all. And *I* think it's good. Don't you think this is a really dumb-looking donkey?"

More kids started laughing.

Mr. Dash swiveled his head and glared around the room. "Class," he growled, "be quiet."

The room went dead silent. The art teacher was over six feet tall, with broad shoulders, huge hands, and a bright red beard that covered most of his face. No student ever disobeyed an order from Mr. Dash.

With one exception. Because Clay kept talking.

"I mean, c'mon, Mr. Dash. If you'd said, 'Whatever you do, don't draw a donkey wearing glasses today,' then I wouldn't have. But you didn't say that. So I drew a donkey wearing glasses. Who has a mustache."

Then Clay held up his drawing so everyone else in the class could see he was telling the truth.

It was all true. He had made a picture of a donkey with a mustache who was wearing a sport coat and a striped necktie and dark-rimmed glasses—a donkey that looked remarkably stupid. And funny.

But not a single kid laughed.

Because that long-faced donkey looked like someone, a real person—a man every kid in the room was scared of. Except for one.

Clay had drawn a donkey that looked like Mr. Kelling, the principal of Truman Elementary School.

CHAPTER TWO

ON PURPOSE

Clay knew what he was doing. He'd made the drawing on purpose, he'd let Mr. Dash see it on purpose, and then he'd held it up on purpose so everyone else in the classroom could see it too—and that last action was important.

Because now Mr. Dash couldn't just give him a scolding and move on—no way.

Every student in the class had *seen* the principal looking like a stupid jackass, and once those kids got out of the art room, they would tell all their friends about the hilarious drawing Clay Hensley had made. And sooner or later, the principal would hear about it—he would. And, when Mr. Kelling *did* hear about it, he would come stomping down the hall to the art room, his eyes blazing and his mustache twitching, and he would demand to know why Mr. Dash hadn't *done* something about that terrible boy and his terrible behavior.

So Mr. Dash had to do something. Clay was sure about that.

Would the art teacher keep him after school? Clay didn't care—as long as he got home in time for dinner. Mitch was going to be there tonight, and in a way, the more stuff that happened now, the better. He'd have that much more of a story to tell his big brother. Detention in the art room? No problem.

But Clay didn't think that was going to happen. It was Friday, a warm, sunny October day, and he had seen Mr. Dash ride his big motorcycle into the school parking lot this morning. It was perfect weather for cruising, and the back roads of Belden County were going to be beautiful this afternoon. The art teacher would *not* be staying late for a detention, not today.

Clay was pretty sure about that, too.

"Give me the drawing."

Clay handed it over, and Mr. Dash walked to his desk and took a large tan envelope out of a drawer. He slipped the drawing inside and sealed the envelope with tape. Then he picked up a marker and wrote on the front.

He handed the envelope to Clay and said, "Take this to the office and give it to the secretary. And then wait there until Mr. Kelling talks to you himself. Understand?"

Clay nodded, his face blank and serious. He didn't want to be disrespectful toward Mr. Dash. He was a pretty good guy. He was just doing what he had to, that's all.

As Clay picked up his backpack and headed for the door, every other kid was watching, studying his face, trying to imagine why he had made that drawing—and trying to imagine what Mr. Kelling was going to do when he saw it.

BriAnne whispered to James, and in the quiet room everyone heard her.

"Clay's really gonna get it this time."

CHAPTER THREE

TO SEE AND BE SEEN

G etting from the art room to the office wasn't going to take long—maybe a minute. But Clay wasn't in a hurry.

He stopped at the water fountain and took a long drink.

He studied all the artwork in the display cases, including two of his own drawings.

He went into the boys' room and stood in front of the big mirror and combed his long black hair into three different styles. Then he combed it all back to his regular look—parted straight down the middle and tucked behind his ears, the same way Mitch wore his. Even though Mitch was seven years older, the two of them looked a lot alike, almost like twins—everybody said so.

As he came out of the washroom, a voice boomed, "Hey, get to the office *now*!"

Mr. Dash was standing outside the art room.

Clay waved and then ducked around the corner into the front hall. But he didn't go toward the office, not yet. He waited ten seconds, then peeked back around the corner.

Mr. Dash was gone, so Clay scooted across the open intersection and trotted halfway down the east hallway to the music room. He knew Hank Bowers had chorus now. He stood in the open doorway, pointing and nodding at other kids until they finally got his friend's attention. Then he made faces and scratched his armpits like a chimpanzee until Hank laughed out loud and got yelled at by Mrs. Norris.

Clay hooted, "Woo-wooh!" into the doorway, then ran back across the hallway intersection and arrived at the office just as the bell rang to end fourth period.

But he didn't go *into* the office. He kept away from the wide windows and leaned up against the tiled wall.

In his mind Clay began composing how he was going to tell Mitch about all of this later on. First was getting the idea for the drawing, then forcing Mr. Dash to send him to the principal with it, then goofing around in the empty halls and taking his own sweet time getting to the office. So far, it was a pretty good story.

Of course, he might also have to tell the story to his mom and dad, especially if things turned sour with the principal. But as long as he hadn't been punching kids or breaking windows, his folks weren't going to get too upset. They never had before—at least, not since second grade or so. And who knows? His dad might even get a good laugh out of it.

A lot of the sixth graders were heading back from art and music now, and they were going to have to walk right past the office on their way to lunch. Clay had placed himself in the perfect spot to see everyone—and be seen.

He especially wanted the kids from his art class to see him standing there, to see that he hadn't even gone into the office yet, to see that the envelope with the drawing was still in his hand, still taped shut. They'd all be talking about his drawing, he knew they would. They'd be talking about what BriAnne had whispered to James: "Clay's really gonna get it this time."

And thinking about *that* brought the perfect

smile to his face, the smile he wanted everyone to see, a smile that said, Yeah, that's right—I'm doing this *my* way, same as always.

While he was enjoying that thought and nodding at the kids who waved or caught his eye, Hank came up from his left and punched him on the arm.

"*That's* for gettin' me yelled at in chorus!"

Clay grinned and turned, then made a quick move like he was going to punch back. But he didn't. "It was worth it," he said.

Hank smiled, agreeing. "What're you waitin' here for?" he said. "Let's go eat."

Clay shook his head. "Can't. Gotta go see the warden."

"Yeah? What'd you do now?"

"I made a little drawing, that's all."

Clay opened the brown envelope—just ripped off the tape, pulled out the picture, and held it up.

Hank's eyes bugged out so far that Clay thought they were going to pop and squirt slime everywhere.

"Oh, *man*!" he gasped. "You are so *dead*! Mr. K. seen that yet?"

Clay snorted. "What do *you* think?"

Hank stared at the drawing, then at Clay, and then suddenly seemed terrified, speechless.

"Yeah," said Clay with a grin, "after *that* jack-ass gets a good look at *this* jackass, I don't think I'll be hangin' out in the halls much, do you?"

Hank shook his head, and then kept on shaking it, both eyebrows up as far as they would go.

Clay started laughing, and when he noticed some other kids looking their way and pointing, he laughed even harder.

"Please hand that to me."

The deep voice was right behind him.

Clay stopped laughing. He turned around and gave the paper to Mr. Kelling. The principal looked at the drawing—and Hank slid three steps sideways and hurried toward the lunchroom.

The principal glanced up from the picture straight into Clay's eyes.

"My office. Now."

Clay nodded and walked toward the doorway, being sure to keep a cool, carefree look on his face.

But inside, he was actually grinning. This thing was shaping up just right—and he couldn't wait to tell Mitch all about it.

CHAPTER FOUR

THE FOLDER

Mrs. Ormin loved her job. She and one part-time helper did the work of five people every school day. They dealt with the daily attendance, the substitute teachers, the before- and after-school programs, the PTO activities, the bus schedules, the constant correspondence and record keeping, and a never-ending flow of small and large emergencies. She accounted for every penny that came into or went out of the school. She ordered and tracked all the office and classroom supplies, and she managed the principal's busy calendar. Mrs. Ormin had been the school secretary for nineteen years, and thanks to her, the office at Truman Elementary School was like a calm harbor, a safe haven of order and efficiency.

Six years ago, shortly after Mr. Kelling became principal, the state board of education had issued a new rule: "Whenever a pupil is sent to a school officer for discipline, a second adult shall be present to observe and take notes." And that rule had forced Mrs. Ormin into the least favorite part of her job.

Since then, she had watched dozens and dozens of little children sit there in front of Mr. Kelling's desk and burst into tears. He didn't mean to make them cry—she was sure of that. But she could see why the kids got upset. The principal was a person with a lot of nervous energy, and he was always tapping a pencil or drumming his fingers or shaking his foot. It made him seem impatient. And when he had to discipline children, his voice usually got too loud. That twitchy little mustache of his didn't help either—she could tell the children always stared at it when he was talking.

The odd thing was, he was terrific at working with the teachers. Mr. Kelling knew how to keep everything bright and upbeat and friendly—even when he was constantly insisting that everyone had to become better and better at teaching. Most of the staff liked and respected him. And he was also good at working with parents and the school committee and all the other people he had to speak with every day.

But talking to one child, one young boy or girl? He never seemed to find the right tone. He would perch uncomfortably on the front edge of his chair, leaning forward, staring across his desk. Mr. Kelling blinked a lot, and his dark-rimmed glasses made his eyes seem extra large and bright. And seven times out of ten, a child would start to cry. Or whimper. Or moan and wail. Mrs. Ormin kept a box of tissues handy.

The students always survived, of course, and they always told their friends how horrible it was to get sent to the principal's office. Mrs. Ormin agreed. She disliked it almost as much as the kids did . . . *except* when Clay Hensley showed up.

And here he was again. Was this his third time this month? Or was it the fourth? She couldn't recall. What was the school going to do when this boy moved on to the junior high next year? Heave a deep sigh of relief, probably. But she felt pretty sure that *she* would miss him—secretly, of course. He certainly kept things interesting.

Mrs. Ormin's chair was to the right of the principal's desk, and she sat with Clay's student file folder on her lap. She also had her notepad and three sharpened pencils. She always brought extra pencils when Clay met with the principal.

She looked at her watch. The principal had kept the boy waiting four minutes so far. She had seen Mr. Kelling do this before. He kept children waiting so they had time to think about their mistakes, time to realize how sorry they were. It had never worked on Clay before, and it wasn't working today.

He sat there in the hard plastic chair in front of the broad desk, perfectly calm, looking around the office as if he didn't have a care in the world. He almost seemed happy. *This* child had never shed a tear in the principal's office, hadn't even come close. And how many times had he sat there in that chair?

Mrs. Ormin started to do the math. *Let's say he's been sent to the office, on average, four times a month . . . so that's four multiplied by nine months in each school year . . . and he's in sixth grade now, and he's been a regular visitor since the middle of kinder—*

"Hey, Mrs. Ormin, is that a new picture?" Clay pointed at a framed photo on the wall. "Looks like the principal's kids are growing up, huh?" He gave her a big smile.

Mrs. Ormin didn't smile back, but it took some effort. The rascal could be so charming. But goodness, what a troublemaker. She glanced down at Clay's student folder. It was almost two inches thick. The only other folder that had gotten anywhere near this size was the one filled up by Clay's big brother, Mitchell Hensley. With Mitchell, it had usually been yelling or arguing or pushing or shoving or even fighting that had gotten him sent to the office.

The two boys looked a lot alike, but Clayton's brand of troublemaking was different. Yes, he had that same lack of fear Mitchell had shown, but Clay almost never seemed angry. And with Clay, there was so much cleverness in his mischief, and such a wide variety of offenses. It was almost . . . inspiring.

She smiled to herself. In a way, she was proud of Clayton's folder. After all, she had written most of what was in it. It certainly wasn't literature—she knew that. But it still made pretty good reading. It was more like journalism . . . or history. Definitely nonfiction. This folder was her masterpiece.

Ignoring the boy in the chair, Mrs. Ormin set her pencils and notepad on the edge of the principal's desk and opened up the file, flipping back through the years. She stopped at the printed transcript from one of Clay's early meetings with the principal.

Thursday, October 17
10:25 a.m.
Disciplinary meeting with Alfred Kelling, Principal
Witnessed and recorded by Claire Ormin

Student: Clayton Hensley, grade one
Sent to the office by Mrs. Gallio
Infraction: Running in the halls

"Can I look at those little squiggles she always makes? What's that called again?"

"It's called shorthand. Now, Clayton, I have to tell you that I am not one bit happy to hear about—"

"Look! That stuff you just said? It's all squiggles now! How come she always does that when I'm here?"

"Mrs. Ormin uses shorthand because it's a way to write that's faster than regular handwriting. She's writing down every word we say. Clayton, you are here today—"

"How come she doesn't just make a recording?"

"Because Mrs. Ormin has to be here in the office with us anyway, and she knows how to write shorthand. Now, the last time we talked you prom—"

"She's got to be here with us every single time? How come?"

"It's just a rule, for everyone's protection. Clayton, your teacher has reported—"

"Does Mrs. Ormin know karate or something?"

"Karate? I don't see what that has to do with—"

"For protection. Or maybe kung fu? She doesn't carry a gun, does she?"

"No, it's not that kind of protection. It's just a rule. Your teacher tells me that—"

"How come you don't teach everybody in the whole school to write fast like she does? I write really, really slow. Can she write down every single thing, even if I talk fast? How about if I talk faster and faster and faster and faster and faster and faster and superfaster and superfaster—Hoosh! Look at her go! She's still keeping up! Can I try that squiggle stuff?"

"We're not here to talk about shorthand, Clayton, so be quiet and listen. We're here today because your teacher informs me that you have been told six times this week that you are not allowed to run in the halls, and you keep on running. So Mrs. Gallio sent you here to talk to me."

"I like Mrs. Gallio. She's nice. She's really tall. She any good at basketball? I got a cousin named Baldwin, he's six foot three, except he can't play basketball worth a spit. Hoosh! Isn't that stupid? Is Mrs. Gallio mad at me?"

"No, she simply wants—"

"Good. I like Mrs. Gallio. She's tall. And nice."

"I like her too. But tell me, Clay, do you think it would be good if all the children ran in the halls?"

"Not sure. Anybody ever try? Maybe it'd be okay. How about if tomorrow everybody runs in the halls all they want? But they have to be quiet. And I bet nobody'll be late! Ever think about that? Might be okay."

"But you see, Clay, running in the halls is against the rules."

"That's what the man said at the supermarket yesterday."

"You were running in the supermarket?"

"Yup, except that's not why I got yelled at. I ate a grape. To see if it was sour. This guy yelled at me, said it was against the rules. So stupid! You want some grapes, and you buy them and get all

23

the way home, and then they're sour! What then? It's like the store tricks you into buying the sour ones. Doesn't anybody taste the grapes? And what about when the store buys 'em from the farmer? Maybe the farmer has the same rule—no tasting the grapes! Stupid rule. Some things you don't have to taste. Like that goulash yesterday? You just sniff and you know it's gonna taste like dog food. Ever eat dog food? I did, but just that once. Tasted like that goulash smelled. But grapes don't smell much, unless you squish 'em."

"Clay, we're talking here about running in the halls, and I am telling you that it's against the rules. What if everyone in the whole school ran together in one hallway, do you think that would be safe?"

"'Course not. Be too crowded. Who said anything about that? I sneak out of the room and run around the halls all by myself. There's lots of room."

"But I just told you it's against the rules, Clayton. And it's also against the rules to sneak out of your classroom."

"How come Mrs. Gallio has to look at me? She hears me running, she should just look somewhere else until she can't hear me anymore."

24

"Now listen carefully. Are you saying that if there's a red light on a highway, and it's the middle of the night, and there are no other cars coming, then it's all right if you just drive your car right through that red light? Even if it's against the law?"

"What car? I don't have any car. I can't even drive yet. Hoosh!—I mean, I was just running in the hall, and there wasn't any red lights, and I didn't bump anybody. I never do."

"Clay, what I'm telling you is that you have to obey the rules—all the rules—and stop running in the halls, and also stop sneaking out of your room, and if you keep on doing things like this, then you're going to get another note put into your folder."

"My folder? What folder? I don't have any folder."

"It's the school's folder, Clayton. It's where we keep your records."

"Records? Like my mom's Elvis records?"

"No, no. We keep information. In your folder."

"Stuff about me?"

"That's right. Records about everything you do here at school."

"Like that time when I threw up in the boys' room—is that in my folder?"

"No, the record folder—"

"So you don't really put every single thing in there."

"No, not every single thing. Mostly the very good things and the very bad things."

"I done any very good things yet?"

"Clayton, I just want you to remember that you have to stop this running—"

"You got *all* the bad things in there? Like when I gave that dead toad a turn on the sliding board? Is that in there?"

"Yes, it is."

"How about when I opened the back door on the school bus?"

"That was very dangerous, Clayton. I'm glad no one was hurt."

"Me too. I know that was bad. My football rolled right out and bounced off a mailbox and then got run over by a truck. And since you and me talked about that, I never opened another bus door, and I'm not going to."

"Good. Because that was a very bad thing, and yes, that's in your folder too."

"So really . . . it's my rap sheet."

"Your rap sheet? No, it's—"

"Like my uncle Loomis has. All the bad stuff

he's ever done. I saw it. He stole three cars. He says his rap sheet's as long as his arm, but it's not. It's just a piece of paper with words on it. How long is a piece of paper? Hold out your arm. I bet my arm's almost as long as yours."

"Clayton, I don't want to see you in here again."

"Can I come back if I do something really good?"

"What I mean is that I want you to—"

"Because I like it in here. I like that picture of the president, too. You ever talk to him?"

"Clayton, I mean I don't want Mrs. Gallio to tell me you've been running in the halls again."

"I don't want her to tell on me again either."

"So that means you have to stop the running, Clayton. All right?"

"I guess so. I'll see if I can."

"I know you can, Clayton. You can stop running in the halls if you want to."

"I'm a good runner, and I don't bump things or fall down much, and when you run, you get places faster. It's good to get places faster."

"But not if it's against the rules."

"Who makes up the rules?"

"Lots of people. People who care about keeping everybody safe. You want everyone to be safe, don't you, Clayton?"

"Sure I do—I'm not stupid."

"I know that. You're very smart, Clayton. And you can understand that it's smart not to break rules and run in the halls. It makes the school safer."

"But also slower."

"But you *are* going to stop the running in the halls, right, Clayton?"

"I'm going . . . to try. But I might mess up. I mess up a lot. I really wish I could write fast like she does."

Student returned to class 10:33 a.m.

Mrs. Ormin flipped forward through the folder, looking for fourth grade. That had been quite a year for Clay. She wanted to read about the time he got sent to the office for collecting all the uneaten cheese at lunch, and then making it into a statue of a . . .

"Clayton, Mrs. Ormin—sorry to keep you waiting."

Mr. Kelling walked around his desk and sat down, then slid up onto the front edge of his chair. He leaned forward and turned to the secretary. "Do you need a moment?"

She thought, *You know perfectly well I have been waiting here with this boy for the past nine minutes.*

"No," she said, "I'm all set."

It was time to add a new chapter to her master-piece.

CHAPTER FIVE

MITCH

C lay kept his mouth shut that night at dinner, except when he was eating. It was a great meal—a huge platter of fried chicken, a big bowl of mashed potatoes, some green beans, hot rolls, and three kinds of soda. He and his little sister, Anne, had set the table in the dining room, and his older sister, Janie, had helped with the cooking. The family dinner was in honor of Mitch coming home.

Dad and Mitchell were doing most of the talking.

"So, they treat you okay over there in Belden?"

Mitchell answered with his mouth full. "Wasn't exactly a vacation, but it could have been a lot worse, that's for sure. Met a couple of pretty good guys, plus a bunch of rotten ones." He took a gulp

of root beer, then burped a little. "You remember Ronnie Clark, great big guy used to play nose tackle on my high school team? He got busted for stealing six cases of work boots from his father-in-law's store, and it was his second offense. He's in there for another whole year, unless he can get parole. And his marriage is over too. Hasn't turned him mean, though, at least not yet. Good to see him—but I'd have to say that was the only good thing about the last month or so."

Clay knew what his brother was talking about. Almost two months ago Mitch got pulled over for speeding on Route 113 over near Belden. Instead of paying the two-hundred-dollar ticket, he went to court and tried to talk his way out of it. The judge didn't believe his excuses, so Mitchell got mad and started shouting. The judge told him to be quiet, and Mitch kept yelling and then knocked over a chair. So the judge charged him with con-tempt of court and locked him up for thirty days in the Belden County Jail. He'd had to pay the speeding ticket, a hundred-dollar fine for con-tempt, plus another hundred and fifty dollars in court fees.

Clay started working on his fourth drumstick, happy just to eat and listen. He'd get his chance to ask questions later. Mitchell was broke, so he was going to be living at home awhile, sleeping on the bottom bunk in his old room again. At bedtime Clay'd probably get to hear all the stuff Mitch wouldn't want to say with Mom and Dad and the girls around.

His mom said, "Your friends have been calling all day—six messages on the machine when I got home from work."

"Yeah," Clay added, "and a bunch of new texts came in on your cell phone today too—but I didn't read any of 'em."

Mitchell smiled at him. "Gonna have to get a phone of your own now, aren't you? I want that back just as soon as you get all the chicken grease off your fingers. And if you ran up my bill, I'll be coming after your allowance, you hear?"

Their mother went on, "Well, I imagine your friends all want you to go out and whoop it up tonight."

Clay could tell how she felt about that idea.

"Don't worry, Mom," Mitchell said. "I'm staying in—don't care if it is a Friday night. Maybe we can watch a movie on TV."

Dad dropped a thigh bone onto his plate. "That Judge Parker?" he snarled. "*There's* a piece of work."

Clay knew what was coming next. They all did. His dad had some history with the local judge, and they'd heard his opinions about the man before.

"I ever tell you how we both used to deliver the *Post-Dispatch* back when we were kids over in Turnbull? He did east of Main Street, and I covered the west side. Always bragging about how his route was better than mine—a real stuck-up, snot-nosed kid. He got four times the tips I got at Christmas, all those rich east siders. Bet he got a big laugh about throwing a Hensley boy in jail. I beat him up once when we were kids, and if I got him alone in some dark alley right now, why, I'd knock the livin' daylights—"

"Trent Hensley! You stop that!" His wife looked like she was going jump right across the table at him. "I will not have you talking like that in front of these children!"

Mitchell took a last gulp of soda, then bent the can between his thumb and fingers. "Truth is, Dad, I don't blame Judge Parker," he said quietly. "I mouthed off pretty bad in court. He could've given me sixty days in jail, or even ninety. I've got no gripe with him. It was my own fault—all of it."

Clay stared at his big brother. Everyone else

did too, all the way around the kitchen table. That didn't sound like Mitch talking, it just didn't.

Mom said, "Glad to hear someone in this family making sense for a change. Clayton, help Anne and Janie clear away while I serve up the ice cream. I got you that double-fudge chunk, Mitchell."

"That's great, Mom. Thanks."

Clay stood up and collected a stack of plates and the bowl of chicken bones, and then snuck a quick look over at Mitch. He still wasn't used to seeing his brother with his hair so short. But he was still the same person, no matter what he looked like now. He was tall and strong and almost twenty years old. He was still the toughest guy around.

Clay was pretty sure his brother was just saying all that nicey-nice stuff to make Mom feel better. He'd probably already figured out a way to get even with that judge—maybe trash his yard some night, or tag the guy's car. Because nobody messed with Mitch Hensley and got away with it—nobody.

He'd probably hear all about it at bedtime, along with everything else that happened at the jail. Maybe there'd been some big fights, some real knuckle-busters.

Clay couldn't wait to tell Mitch about his run-in with the principal. And when he showed him that drawing? That would be sweet.

It was great to have him around the house again. Really great.

CHAPTER SIX

WAKE-UP CALL

Clay was in the upper bunk fighting to stay awake. He could hear Mitch outside on the back porch, talking on the phone, his voice mostly soft. Probably talking to some girl.

Clay yawned so hard it hurt his jaw muscles. He hadn't had a moment alone with his brother all night. Janie had gone to the mall with her boyfriend, but everyone else had watched a Clint Eastwood movie in the living room. Their folks had slept through most of it, except his dad woke up when he smelled the popcorn. It was almost midnight now.

The large bedroom he and Mitch shared had been used as the family room back before Anne was born. The TV was out in the living room now, but some of the old furniture had stayed behind. Clay had left the lamp on over by the couch to help keep himself awake. He stifled another yawn. How long was Mitchell going to talk? He'd already been out there twenty minutes.

He must have dozed off, but his eyes popped open when the latch on the bedroom door clicked shut.

Mitchell sat on the couch and bent over to pull off his shoes. Clay noticed again how short his hair was, the way he'd had to wear it back when he was on the high school football team. They probably did that to him at the jail.

"Hey," said Clay.

"Hey there, little man. Didn't mean to wake you up—sorry."

"No, I wasn't asleep." Clay propped himself up on one elbow. "I wanted to wait up and talk."

"Yeah? About what?"

"Just stuff. And what it was like being in jail."

"Not much to tell about that," said Mitchell. "It's a big building with a lot of cages and a lot of angry people, and that includes most of the guards. And it's dangerous. That's the first thing Ronnie Clark told me. Me and him, we stuck pretty close together, looked out for each other. I'm glad he was there. And now, I'm glad I'm here."

Clay frowned. "Was jail sort of like it is in the movies?"

"Prob'ly depends on which movies you're talkin' about. But mostly it's lots worse. Because every minute you're there, you know it's for real. It's not some movie. You're really there, and if you look at the wrong guy the wrong way, he might take a swing at you or find some other way to mess you up. There's nothing good about it. I'm not going back. Ever."

Clay was quiet a minute or two. He wasn't used to hearing Mitch sound like that, like he was scared of something.

Mitch leaned back into the couch cushions. "So what've you been up to the last month or so?"

Clay shrugged. "Not much."

"School's okay?"

"Yeah, mostly. Except I went to the office today—but I got sent on purpose."

Mitchell tilted his head. "Really? How come?"

"Look on your cell phone . . . you're gonna love this."

Mitch pulled the phone from his back pocket.

"Okay," said Clay. "Now check out the newest picture in the photo stack—see it? That's the principal."

Mitchell nodded slowly. "Yup. I met him last year when Mom and Dad were in Chicago—the time you and that kid bumped heads in gym class. So . . . the principal saw this picture?"

Clay grinned. "Yup. I drew it in art class today, then I made sure the teacher saw it. And he sent me to the office—he didn't have much choice about it."

"Why'd you do it?"

"Mr. Kelling. He stopped me in the cafeteria on Monday, made me tuck in my shirt—can you believe that? Right there, with everyone watching me. Made a big show of it. Gave a whole speech about the school dress code. So today, I got him back. I told him I think he's a dumb jackass, which he is—except I didn't say it out loud."

Mitchell nodded slowly, looking at the picture again. "What'd he do about this?"

"Nothing—not one thing." Clay grinned down at his brother. "I had a perfect alibi."

"For this?" said Mitchell.

"Yup—I told him how when we studied the Civil War, we looked at all these cartoons from old newspapers. And I told him how this one art-ist made President Lincoln look like a huge, hairy ape. I said I was trying that out in art class, making a cartoon of a real person. And then the art teacher saw it, and he sent me to the office before I could explain I was just doing something I learned about in social studies."

"And the guy *believed* that?"

Clay laughed. "'Course not. But he couldn't prove anything. So he just said I 'should use better judgment.' But you're never gonna guess what Kelling did then."

"What?"

"He said he'd give me ten bucks for the picture, asked me if I would *sign* it. Said he wanted to get it framed and keep it in his office." Clay grinned. "So I signed it."

"Did you take the money?"

"Sure I did. It was like he really thought it was funny. But I know he got my message—that he's a *major* jerk."

"Hey," Mitchell said, "come here a second— I've got somethin' for you."

Clay hopped down from the upper bunk and walked to the couch.

"What?" he said.

Mitchell shot out a hand and gave him a sharp tap on the side of the head. "That's for being a jerk yourself." Quick as a snake, he cuffed Clay again on the other side of his head. "And that's to make sure I've got your attention. Are you listening to me?"

Clay nodded sullenly. His eyes were watering, more from hurt feelings than being smacked.

"I'm only sayin' this once. Starting Monday, you're gonna stop bein' a goof-off at school. You're gonna be nice, and do good work, and not get in any more trouble. You're gonna get good grades and show respect. You're gonna do all the stuff that I never did—and do things right, the smart way. You understand what I'm saying?"

Clay pressed his lips together.

The hand flashed out again, and as Clay flinched, Mitchell stopped midswing. He reached out and grabbed his brother by both shoulders. They were eye to eye.

"Look," said Mitchell, "being in jail was the worst thing ever, the worst. I'm never going back and you're not even gonna get close." He paused. "I shouldn't have hit you. And I'm not doing that again. But I don't want you to mess up anymore. I'm gonna do things different now too—I am. We can kind of do this together, okay? I'm sorry I hit you. But I'm serious about this, that's all. I'm serious about it. Now go on, get back in bed."

As Clay reached the ladder to the upper bunk, Mitchell said, "Hey, toss me that pillow from down below. I'm sleeping over here. Been in a bottom bunk for thirty nights, and I don't want to wake up that way tomorrow."

Clay grabbed the pillow and threw it at him, hard.

Mitchell looked at him, started to say something, then reached up and switched off the lamp.

"Get some sleep. We're going to the mall tomorrow."

"The mall? How come?"

"Just go to sleep."

A minute later, Clay heard a snort, and then long, slow breathing—just like that, Mitch was sound asleep.

Not him. Clay lay on the upper bunk, wide awake in the dark.

Mitch wasn't kidding around, he could tell that. But all that stuff he'd said about school? That was, like . . . crazy.

It was probably just the time in jail making Mitch act like this. He'd get over it. A couple of days around home and he'd calm down again. He'd forget all about that stuff, and everything would get back to normal.

Yeah, everything was going to be okay.

TRUST

Clay avoided his brother all Saturday morning. Then around two thirty he heard Mitch in the living room watching TV. He went in and sat down next to him on the couch. It was a heist movie, and a gang of jewel thieves were making plans to break into a museum.

When a commercial came on, Clay said, "So . . . are we still going to the mall today? Like you said last night?"

Mitch muted the TV and turned to look at him. "That depends."

"On what?" said Clay.

"Depends on whether you trust me or not."

Clay made a face. "What're you talking about?"

"It's a simple question," Mitch said. "Do you trust me, or not?"

"Yeah, of course I trust you," said Clay. "But what's that got to do with going to the mall?"

"You remember what I said last night, about school?"

"Yeah . . . ," said Clay. He also remembered getting smacked upside the head. Twice.

"Well," Mitch went on, "I don't think it's gonna be easy—to change and everything. And I'm not even sure you can cut it, especially if you think it's a stupid idea. 'Cause that's what I saw in your face last night. You thought what I said was stupid. So . . . you don't trust me."

Clay gulped. "I just . . . I don't know what you're all freaked out about. I mean, *you're* the one who got in trouble and went to jail, and then all of a sudden *I'm* the one who's got to do everything different? That's just . . ."

"Stupid?" said Mitch. He turned back to the TV. The movie was on again. The leader of the gang was passing out maps and tools and ski masks.

The room felt empty, hollow. Over the past couple of years it was like he and Mitch had become more than brothers—real friends. Even went camping in the Ozarks for a whole week, just the two of them. And now? Mitch was a hundred miles away.

Clay took a deep breath. "Like . . . what do I actually have to do?"

Mitch kept his eyes on the TV. "Trust me. Trust that I know what's good for you, even if it feels stupid. Because you're gonna be in junior high next year, and then it'll be high school, *real* soon. And the way you're headed right now? It's not good. But if you don't want to listen to me about this stuff, then just go ahead and do whatever you want. On your own."

Mitch clicked the sound on. The thieves were piling into two cars, huge black SUVs. The doors slammed and the engines roared and they blasted out into the city traffic.

Clay stared at the screen, but he barely saw it. He was remembering that camping trip.

About three days in, the trail came to a stream. It was a tiny blue line on the map, but the actual thing was running fast and cold, swelled by recent rain. They'd found the narrowest spot and Mitch tossed both their packs over. Then, with a running leap, he made it across, no problem.

"C'mon, Clay!"

"It's too wide!"

He'd had to yell above the noise of rushing water.

Mitch stood on the far bank, holding out a hand. "You can do it—just get a good head start and jump. Don't worry, I'll catch you!"

So he had backed up as far as he could. He ran, took a flying leap, and landed on a wet rock. His feet slipped, but Mitch grabbed his arm and pulled. It was over in three seconds. One boot was full of water, but he'd made it.

Clay got up off the couch.

"Okay," he said.

Mitch looked at him. "'Okay' what?"

"Okay, I trust you."

Mitch turned off the TV and stood up. "Good." He smiled and made a half turn, tapping his right shoulder. "You want to take a free shot right here—for me slappin' you last night?"

Clay grinned. "Nah . . . I'll wait till you're not ready for it."

Mitch laughed. "Fair enough. Okay, little man. Let's go to the mall."

CHAPTER EIGHT

LONG MORNING

When Clay got on the school bus Monday morning, he walked toward his favorite seat at the very back, and all the other kids scattered just like always. But when he sat down, a couple dozen faces were aimed his way, staring.

He eyeballed two fifth-grade boys. "What're *you* lookin' at?"

They turned away instantly, and so did everyone else.

But Clay knew what they were looking at. Most likely, it was the haircut.

Mitchell had promised not to smack him anymore, but at the barbershop on Saturday afternoon it had taken some serious threats to keep Clay in that chair. When the deed was done, two years'

worth of hair lay on the floor. Sure, he still had three inches left on top, and he could still part his hair down the middle, sort of. But the sides? Short. To Clay, it seemed like he was bald, plus his neck was cold. And with his ears sticking out, he felt like Mr. Potato Head.

Horrible.

Of course, the kids on the bus also could have been looking at his clothes. No one had ever seen Clay wearing anything except jeans and a T-shirt or a hoodie—until today.

Saturday's shopping trip with Mitchell had been a nightmare. Clay had followed his big brother around the mall, watching him pick out clothes.

Clay had rebelled. "You're kidding, right? I'm supposed to wear stuff like *that*? I'm gonna look like some loser in a back-to-school ad!"

But Mitch had said, "Look, I told you it wasn't gonna be easy. Because you've gotta send a big message to everybody that the old Clay Hensley is gone. It's the right move. Trust me."

So there he was at the back of the bus, wearing a gray and green flannel shirt with a folded collar and little white buttons up the front. The shirt was tucked into baggy tan khakis held up by a brown belt.

His black Velcro high-tops, the ones with the designs he'd made with permanent marker all around the white rubber edges? Gone. But at least he'd been able to talk Mitch out of some ugly brown leather lace-ups. They had compromised on a pair of completely boring black sneakers.

Ridiculous.

Clay also had a new blue backpack, and Mitchell had laid down the law about that, too. "No weird drawings on this thing, okay? And no safety pins along the edges, no bumper stickers on the back, no flames on the sides, no custom paint job, no nothing—you got it?"

When he walked into his homeroom, Clay felt like an alien. Everyone treated him that way too, sneaking peeks when they thought he wasn't looking. They didn't know whether to laugh or be afraid. He didn't blame them.

Hank skidded into the room just before the final bell, took one look at Clay, cracked this huge grin, and said, "I get it, I get it—early Halloween costume, right? That is completely *awesome*!"

Clay didn't even try to explain. He just gritted his teeth and shook his head. He sat down in his assigned seat, got out his notebook and a pencil, and began checking over his math homework—he had done every single problem.

When Hank saw him do all that, he stopped laughing. "Hey—what're you *doing*? And why do you look like . . . like *that*? Is this because of that thing on Friday with Mr. K.? Like, did you have to go to special counseling over the weekend or something?"

Clay was tempted to start talking like he was a brainwashed robot, which would have been funny—Hank would totally freak out. But he used his normal voice. "I'm just going to school today—*school*, that's all. And this is what I look like now. So get used to it."

That was all he said.

Apart from the way he felt about his appearance, homeroom included a different kind of torture for Clay. Mr. Brighton was absent, and there was a brand-new substitute teacher.

The woman looked like she was about seventeen. She was all nervous and chatty, trying to be way too friendly with the kids. It would have been so much fun to mess with her head—maybe act like he only spoke Russian . . . or maybe he could start crying and tell her how his pet skunk had died yesterday . . . or maybe pretend he was allergic to her makeup, see if he could get her to scrub all of it off her face. He could riff and goof and tumble her head around until she ran screaming out of the room . . . like some other subs had.

But Clay didn't do any of that—he didn't even put a sticky note on her back.

All around him, kids were being stupid and annoying, just like always. Alex started bragging about how he'd gotten this really cool new toothbrush. What a dweeb! Tonia was trying to get Jacob's attention because she thought he was so cute—about as cute as a dead fly. And out of the corner of his eye, Clay saw Lee secretly picking his nose. All these opportunities staring him in the face, and what was he doing? Nothing—because he'd made a promise to his big brother.

He had given Mitch his word that he wouldn't tease anybody, that he wouldn't put anybody down, that he wouldn't make any jokes or rude noises. He had promised not to do *anything* that might get him yelled at, or get him kept after school, or get him sent to the office—or get him suspended or expelled.

By the end of homeroom Clay felt exhausted.

In science class Mrs. Charter started a new unit about water on Earth—the oceans, the water cycle, the growth of deserts, shrinking glaciers—all kinds of stuff. And during a demonstration, Clay could have gotten away with squirting salt water at four or five different kids—but he stopped himself each time.

Then during gym class everyone had to run four laps around the track, and he could have hidden out behind the equipment shed on the far side of the field. That's what Hank and the Miller brothers did, loafing around until the final half lap. Clay made himself play by the rules, and he ran the whole distance.

During fourth-period music Clay had an endless flow of fun ideas. How loud could he sing random words before the teacher told him to knock it off? What would his dusty footprints look like all over the black sweater of the girl sitting in front of him? If he stared cross-eyed at Liam, could he crack him up, maybe get him in trouble? And what if he kept asking Mrs. Norris to play the starting note for the tenor part over and over and over? How many times would she plunk that same note on the piano before she completely lost her temper? The whole period could have been full of adventure and danger and fun.

Clay didn't do any of that. He sat there holding

his songbook, and he opened his mouth wide like Mrs. Norris always said they should, and he sang.

He walked out of the music room and, as usual, he met up with Hank. As they headed toward the cafeteria, Clay felt sort of relieved. He'd survived the bus ride and homeroom, and then he had fought his way through each of his morning classes without goofing off or causing one bit of trouble for anyone.

He actually felt proud of himself—and even better, he knew Mitch would be proud of him too. He started thinking how great it was going to be to tell him all about his first day as the new and improved Clay Hensley.

Really, though, it was a little early to start patting himself on the back. The day was barely half over.

And next came lunch.

CHAPTER NINE

THE TWO MUSKETEERS

Hank had watched Clay all during home-room, and again during second-period gym class. What was he doing with his hair all short—and those clothes?

So far, sixth grade felt like it was going to be the best year ever. Clay and him? They had a blast every day—the guy was awesome, so funny! But today? Clay seemed like a completely different kid.

Hank and Clay had always been pretty good friends, but near the end of fifth grade, one incident had turned them into best buddies.

At lunch one day, Clay had slipped two big slabs of red Jell-O into Donnie Miller's backpack. Later, when Donnie figured out Clay had done it, he got really mad, said he was going to get him back. And the next day during gym, he cornered him.

"You and me, Hensley, out behind the bowling alley after school!"

Clay grinned and said, "Sure. I'll wear my bowling shoes."

Clay was no match for Donnie, and Hank was worried. Donnie had been left back a grade, so he was taller and heavier and stronger. Clay wasn't really a fighter anyway—everybody knew that.

So Hank had stepped in.

He pointed at Donnie's brother Dave, who was also in fifth grade. "How about me and Clay against both you guys?"

The Miller brothers smiled at each other, then nodded. They were famous for fighting as a team—and winning. Hank didn't think he and Clay were going to win the fight or anything, but with the two of them, at least Clay might not get totally pounded.

Clay had taken the bus home first, and then ridden to the bowling alley on his bike. He had shown up actually wearing his dad's bowling shoes.

Around three thirty the four boys squared off among the tall weeds and litter behind the Town and Country Lanes. A handful of other guys and a few of the tough girls had come along to watch.

Donnie Miller didn't waste time. He lowered

his head and charged at Clay. At the last second, Clay jumped aside, but his shin caught Donnie's foot. Donnie clutched at Clay's shirt, and Clay grabbed Donnie's arm. The rest was pure physics— mass, speed, and gravity.

That collision with Clay's shin pitched Donnie forward. He tumbled head over heels and landed flat on his back with a solid *whump*. But to all the kids watching, it looked like Clay had grabbed onto Donnie's arm and flipped him like a kung-fu master.

As Donnie flew past, his foot had bumped Clay's nose, which began gushing blood. Clay barely noticed, and immediately he sat down hard on Donnie's chest, his knees pinning both of the bigger boy's arms to the ground.

He raised a fist, and Donnie said, "Yeah, go ahead, hit me!"

Clay didn't want to. So he just sat there, dripping blood on Donnie's shirt, and watched Hank and Dave circle around, taking swings at each other. But neither of them had any real reason to fight.

The whole event quickly fizzled out, and ten minutes later the four guys were drinking sodas in the bowling alley, laughing and slapping one another on the back.

But Clay's reputation as a tough guy had been established, and word spread through the school. He was an instant legend.

And the two pals, Clay and Hank? They had arrived in sixth grade this fall at the top of the food chain—cool, tough, and funny.

That's why Hank had been watching Clay so closely this morning. If Clay suddenly turned into a goody-goody, it would change everything.

Hank sniffed the air as they got closer to the cafeteria—was that SpaghettiOs? Because SpaghettiOs were always good for some fun.

As weird as Clay looked, and as strange as he'd been acting all morning, Hank was hoping that once they got to lunch, he'd be his regular old self again.

One way or another, he'd find out soon.

CHAPTER TEN

LUNCH EATS BOY

Clay scanned the room as he picked up a tray and headed for the food line. There were about a hundred and fifty kids in the cafeteria, plus two teachers and the custodian. The place sizzled and popped with energy—the kind that only happens in a room where kids outnumber the grown-ups by fifty to one.

Clay smiled, and a slight swagger came back into his step. After keeping such careful watch over every thought and action all morning long, he suddenly felt like he could breathe again. It was time to relax a little, go with the flow.

"Check it out," Hank said, pointing at the green grapes in the salad cooler. "My favorite fruit!"

Clay grinned and nodded. "Yeah, mine too."

He put a cluster on his tray. Then he got a plate of SpaghettiOs, a small paper cup of American cheese cubes, and some vanilla pudding. At the drinks cooler he chose a tall box of organic chocolate milk.

It was a perfectly balanced meal. But it was also an arsenal. He had a tray full of edible missiles—a launchable lunch.

Hank looked around. "Wanna sit over near the fifth graders?"

"Absolutely," said Clay.

Hank's lunch was the same as Clay's, except he'd gotten green Jell-O instead of the pudding. For the first few minutes, they both ate: most of the SpaghettiOs, gulped; most of the grapes, chomped; most of the desserts, gobbled; and all the chocolate milk, chugged. Neither of them touched the cheese cubes.

As Clay ate, he stayed on high alert. He was checking out Mrs. Hale and Ms. Yagin, the two fifth-grade teachers on lunch patrol. They were standing up front by the stage, talking. Not much of a threat. And the custodian wasn't watching anything except the floor, trying to keep up with the worst of the spills.

Hank launched first. The stiff plastic straw that

came with the chocolate milk had a sharp, slanted end. He stuck it into a grape. Gently pinching the grape between his thumb and index finger, he flexed the straw, glanced back over his shoulder, and took careful aim.

"All clear?" he whispered.

"Fire when ready," said Clay.

It was a perfect reverse-release. The grape shot up and over Hank's right shoulder in a low arc, a small green grenade. It smacked against the cheek of a fifth-grade girl sitting four tables away.

"Hey!"

She turned around and accused a boy at the table next to hers.

Both the teachers looked over to see what had caused the commotion, but it died down right away. They resumed their chat.

It was Clay's turn.

He speared a cube of cheese, his favorite missile. Cheese this soft was unpinchable, so it required special launching skill. Touching only the straw, he flexed it, paused, scanned, then released.

The force of the launch was quite good—truly excellent. But the arc was all wrong.

Only two tables away, a large redheaded fifth grader named Tobin took that cheese bomb right in the ear, and it stuck. When he instinctively smacked at the impact point, he forced the soft cheese into his ear.

He stood up and bellowed like an angry bear, then whirled around, looking for his attacker. He stared straight at Clay.

Then he pointed and yelled, "That's not funny, Hensley! It's not funny at all!"

Mrs. Hale agreed with Tobin. She was on the scene in seconds, and the straw on Clay's lunch tray was a dead giveaway—the sharp end was filled with sticky orange cheese.

"Go to the office, Clay. Immediately!"

Ms. Yagin was already leading Tobin out of the cafeteria, headed to the nurse's office for some ear swabbing.

As if he'd jolted awake from a dream, Clay suddenly realized what he'd done—he'd broken his promise to Mitch!

"Please, Mrs. Hale. I'm sorry, really. I shouldn't have done that, I know I shouldn't have, and I'm sorry. And I won't mess up at lunch again for the whole rest of the year—I promise. Please, I won't mess up again."

The teacher glared at him. "I'm supposed to believe that? From you? Just go to the office."

Clay stood up. The kids around him smirked and giggled.

Hank couldn't watch. Clay had just *begged* a teacher not to send him to the office. This was his pal, the guy who always grinned and said, "Sure, no problem." And he was *begging*?

But Hank didn't understand. Because if Clay had thought it would do any good, he would have fallen down onto his knees in front of Mrs. Hale and begged some more.

He knew it wouldn't help.

Clay dropped off his lunch tray and then headed for the office.

CHAPTER ELEVEN

SURPRISES

M rs. Ormin looked over her notes. The meeting in the principal's office had been short but still quite remarkable. In fact, the whole sequence of events had been astonishing. Why, when Clayton had walked into the office from lunch, she'd hardly recognized him—what a dramatic haircut!

She glanced at the clock—still five minutes before fifth period.

Propping up her notebook beside the keyboard, she opened a new document on the computer screen and began to type.

Monday, October 20
12:32 p.m.
Disciplinary meeting with Alfred Kelling, Principal

Witnessed and recorded by Claire Ormin

Student: Clayton Hensley, grade six
Sent to the office by Mrs. Hale
Infraction: Throwing food in cafeteria

"There are four hundred million hungry children
in this world who would love to eat the food you
throw around and waste in our cafeteria. It's a
waste, it's dangerous, and it is not funny, Clayton.
It's never been funny. Do you understand me?"

"Yes."

"And this is the fifth time you've been in here
for discipline this month. So now I have to call
and get your parents to come to school for a
conference."

"Please, Mr. Kelling, I really don't want that to
happen. It would be . . . bad. Really bad."

"Bad? In what way?"

"I . . . I can't say."

"Are you afraid you might be hit by someone,
for example? Because there are laws about that,
and we can—"

"No, no one's going to hit me . . . but I made
a promise. To my big brother. And I forgot and
I messed around at lunch. And I'm sorry, and I

really don't want him to know about this. He . . . he can't know about this. Is there maybe another way I can get punished, besides calling my folks? Can you do that? Because I'm not going to mess up anymore. Not at all."

"That's a lot to believe, Clayton."

"I know . . . but I'm trying not to do that kind of stuff anymore."

"Because of your brother?"

"Yeah, mostly. Because of him. I . . . I'm really going to try to do better. From now on. I really am."

"I'm going to take you at your word, Clayton."

"You are? I mean, that's great!"

"I'm taking you at your word, but how this turns out is going to be up to you. Because if you're not telling me the truth, the consequences will be that much worse later on."

"So . . . you're not going to call my parents?"

"I'm supposed to. You've had five infractions in October. But I'm going to break my own rule. I think this is a special case. But you *will* have to stay after school."

"Um . . . then my brother's still going to find out that I messed up."

"Yes, I see. Then there will be double

70

punishments the next time . . . if there is a next
time."

"Thanks. Really, Mr. Kelling, thanks a lot."

"I have to say it again, Clayton. The way this
turns out depends on you."

"I know."

"All right, then. Off you go."

Student returned to cafeteria at 12:37 p.m.

Scrolling through the document, Mrs. Ormin
felt cheated. The actual conversation in the office
had been loaded with emotion, positively electric.
The words on her computer screen didn't reveal
even half of what had gone on during those three
minutes. She wanted to add information, maybe in
brackets, like the stage directions an author inserts
when writing a play: [*Clay bites his lip, looks down
at his hands, then up into the principal's eyes.*]

The way Clayton's voice sounded when he
begged not to have his parents called? The poor
child had seemed terrified. And the look on Mr.
Kelling's face? She had never seen him so surprised
before—almost shocked, but he had managed to
hide it pretty well.

Then there was that long pause after Clay said

he was really going to try to do better. When Mr. Kelling was deciding what to do, the man sat there completely silent—almost thirty seconds! And the child's face during that time? It was hard to believe this was the same boy who had glared into the principal's eyes just last Friday, and told him that preposterous story about newspaper cartoons. Why, Clay had practically called the principal a jackass, right to his face!

What had happened to this boy over the weekend?

She shook her head. All these children, all these different lives.

The bell rang for fifth period.

Mrs. Ormin saved her document. She'd have to print it out later so the principal could sign it.

Then it would go into Clayton's folder.

CHAPTER TWELVE

CHICKEN OR SOMETHING

Hey, little guy—you keepin' out of trouble?" Mitchell grabbed a banana, then stopped, one hand on the kitchen door.

"Yeah, I am," said Clay. "How about you?"

Mitch held out his arms, showing off his work uniform. He'd found a job making coffee at a doughnut shop. "You think I'm looking for tough-guy action dressed like this?" Then he got serious. "It's not so easy, huh?"

Clay shrugged. "I'm doing okay."

Mitchell smiled at him. "Good man."

This was the first time in four days that they'd been awake in the same room together. Nodding down at his feet, Mitch said, "I see you're switching things up a little, huh?" Clay had on his old Velcro high-tops, the ones with the hand-drawn decorations around the white edges. Also, he was wearing one of his new school shirts unbuttoned down the front, with a black T-shirt underneath.

"Well, yeah," Clay said. "I mean, I can't wear the same thing every single day, can I?"

Mitch nodded. Slowly, his eyes narrowed. "Yeah . . . that makes sense. Listen, I gotta get to work. See you at dinner, okay? Straight home from school—no hangin' around with Hank and them, all right?"

"Yup. See you later."

It had been ten days since he'd been caught flicking cheese in the cafeteria. Clay had been keeping two promises since then—the one to Mitch, and the one he'd made to Mr. Kelling.

Word had gotten around the school that Hensley was on probation, or that he'd turned chicken or something. That first week after the lunchroom business, every guy in sixth grade had tried to pick a fight with him, or at least that's how it had felt to Clay.

Even the younger kids had started mouthing off to him on the school bus. And Tobin, the big fifth grader who took that cheese bomb in the ear? The guy tripped him out on the playground, knocked him flat on his face in the grass. Then he stood there with all his little buddies, laughing. But Clay didn't lose it. He got up, brushed himself off, and walked away. He didn't even say anything—like, *Bet you loved suckin' on those orange Q-Tips in the nurse's office, huh? Mmm—all that cheesy goodness!*

For a full week Clay had spent time each day clenching and then slowly unclenching his fists. And his jaw muscles. Lots of times it had felt like his stomach was strangling itself. Still, nothing had snapped—not yet. He was taking it one day at a time.

And today was Thursday.

Clay left the house about fifteen minutes after Mitchell. He nodded at the two girls who were waiting at his bus stop, and they both said, "Hi, Clay." One of them even smiled a little, which was a surprise—somebody being halfway nice to him.

But by the time the bus pulled up a couple of minutes later, he was ready for the worst. He walked up the steep rubber steps with his face set in a tight mask, prepared to ignore everybody, to not react to anything that came flying his way— whether it was words, rubber bands, or spit wads.

He glanced along the aisle and saw that a gang of fifth graders had claimed the seats in

the back, and part of him wanted to stomp back there and show the little creeps who was boss. Instead, he mentally shrugged and sat down in the first open seat.

It's not important. That's what he told himself. One seat on the bus worked the same as any other.

And sitting there, bouncing around on the hard bench, he realized he wasn't saying that just to make himself feel better. It was actually true, and he knew it. Front seat, back seat, middle seat—it didn't matter. At all.

Nothing happened during the whole ride to school. Nobody tossed stuff at him, nobody teased him, no one insulted him. No one paid any attention to him at all. He was feeling like this might turn out to be a pretty good day.

As the bus turned into the wide school driveway Clay looked out the window. Then he groaned to himself.

Hank and the Miller brothers were waiting on the front sidewalk.

CHAPTER THIRTEEN

HATERS

The school bus squealed to a halt, and when Clay stepped down onto the curb, Hank waved him over.

"Hey, Hensley—I've got some news. That girl who moved here from Florida? Allie says she's got a crush on you. Let's go around back to the field and check her out."

"Yeah!" said Donnie.

Clay smiled. "Sounds like fun . . . except I gotta go to the art room."

"Now? Oh yeah—you're still doing that special project, right?"

Hank was smiling, but Clay caught the way he'd said the word "special."

"Yeah," he said, "Mr. Dash thinks I've got a shot to win something, so I'm goin' for it."

Hank shrugged. "No problem. We can catch Allie 'n' them at lunchtime."

"Yeah," Clay said. "Listen, thanks for waiting for me. See you after chorus, okay?"

"Sure thing," said Hank.

As Clay went in the front doors, he felt Hank watching him. They both knew they weren't going to be hanging around together at lunch.

Hank was the hardest part about all this, even harder than the new clothes—or those fifth graders acting tough. He was a good guy. Clay wanted to stay friends and everything, but it wasn't working out.

Last Saturday, after he'd made a ton of promises to Mitch, he and Hank went to see a new sci-fi movie. They sat up in the balcony, and about halfway through the show, Hank started tossing candy wrappers over the railing, and then popcorn, and then chunks of ice from his drink.

An usher came and threw both of them out. Hank began acting like he wanted to start a fight about it. Clay managed to pull him outside, and then Hank tried to start shoving *him* around. Clay finally got him calmed down, and they waited until Mitch came and drove them home.

It was almost like Hank was turning into *him*,

only meaner. Already it was starting to feel like they weren't very good friends, at least not like they used to be. Clay felt bad about it.

It wasn't like he was making up excuses not to hang out, though. What he'd said about going to the art room? That was true. He'd been spending most of his free time there.

The day after the cheese bomb incident, Mr. Dash had told him about an art contest. He said it was a little late to begin, but that it would be good experience anyway. The contest rules were simple. Before November 10 each participant had to turn in a self-portrait, and it could be created in any medium or artistic style. The contest was open to students in grades six through eight in the Belden County schools. A jury of five faculty members from universities and art schools around St. Louis were going to select one grand prize winner, plus some honorable mentions.

Clay latched on to the idea like it was a life raft.

Mr. Dash set him up with a hall pass and a small work space in the back corner of the art room. There was a square mirror on an easel, a table to draw on, and a chair. A white sheet had been hung over the tall cabinets behind the chair to create a textured background. Clay had marked the floor with pieces of masking tape so he could put the chair in the exact same spot each time. All he had to do was sit in that chair, look in the mirror, and draw what he saw.

Clay was doing his self-portrait in pencil, and Mr. Dash had found him a pad of really good paper. The only bad part was having to spend so much time looking at himself. He still wasn't used to the way he looked. With his hair shorter. And his ears sticking out.

But he understood why the self-portrait idea made for a good art contest. Even though every artist would be creating something completely unique, each would face the same problem. A self-portrait was an interesting challenge.

And Clay was working hard at it. He wanted to have the finished drawing look like a high-quality black-and-white photograph. The last three sessions he had worked on the eyes, and had finally managed to get them looking just right. Overall, he was happy with the way the picture was coming together. Sometimes he was even able to focus only on the lines and the shapes and the shading— and forget whose face it was staring back at him from the mirror.

By the time he got to the art room it was 7:40,

so he'd only have about twenty minutes to work before homeroom.

"Hey, good morning, Clay."

"Hi."

Clay stopped and looked. There were dozens of little pumpkins on the big tables near the windows.

"What're those for?" he asked.

"I'm going to have the third graders decorate them today, and we'll put them on the tables in the cafeteria tomorrow for Halloween."

Mr. Dash was next to the sink, stirring a five-gallon bucket of goo with a meter stick. Clay didn't have to ask about that. It was wallpaper paste for a fifth-grade project—papier-mâché masks.

Papier mâché . . . Clay remembered working with those gummy strips of newspaper last year. And he remembered slipping a bowl of paste onto Todd Tiber's chair just before he sat down—so funny! That had cost him a trip to the office, but it was totally worth it . . . or it had felt that way, back then.

Fifth grade felt like a hundred years ago.

"So," said Mr. Dash, "how's the portrait coming along? Feel like you're making progress?"

"Yeah, I think so. I've got the face started, and I'm working on the background, too, trying to get the texture right. And also the depth."

Mr. Dash turned around and smiled. "Anytime you want another set of eyes to look it over, let me know, okay? There's nothing in the rules that says you can't get a little coaching."

"I'm good for now," Clay said, then quickly added, "But that'll be great—thanks."

"Glad to help out." The teacher went back to his stirring.

Mr. Dash had given him some storage space in the wide metal cabinets along the wall, and Clay slid a drawer open and took out the large pad of Bristol paper. He got his sharpened pencils and gum eraser from his backpack and put them on the table next to the pad, checked the position of the chair, and sat down.

Ready to work.

He glanced up to check that the mirror was tilted correctly. There he was, framed up perfectly, still as funny-looking as he'd been yesterday. He shook his head and gave himself half a smile. He reached for a pencil as he opened the pad to his drawing.

Clay blinked.

Black marks were slashed across the paper.

A dozen or more. Made with a thick marker.

He blinked again, harder.

They were really there. Random scribbles, and a crude mustache drawn below his nose.

He clenched his fists, and the pencil in his right hand broke in two.

The mirror could have broken too. The whole school and everyone in it could have been crushed by the raging red anger that swept through him. He wanted to steam out on the playground and start punching—it didn't matter who had actually done this. He'd pound on everyone, every kid who'd been mean, every kid who'd put him down or sneered or teased him during the last week, all of 'em!

When the crimson fog lifted a little, Clay saw Mr. Dash looking at him.

"You all right?"

"I'm—yeah. I'm okay. Just wish I was a better artist, that's all. I'm gonna start over."

Mr. Dash smiled at him, his teeth bright in his thick beard. "That's how you know you're getting better, when nothing's ever good enough."

Clay nodded and tried to smile back. He couldn't quite do it.

Staring at the ruined drawing, he could almost hear Mitch's voice. *Hey, little man—forget about it, okay? If you go and try to get even, you'll just get yourself in big trouble.*

Yeah, that's what Mitch would say.

Forget about *this*? Never. This deserved some serious payback.

And somebody was gonna get it.

CHAPTER FOURTEEN

BIG LIST

Clay ripped his ruined drawing loose from the pad, folded the stiff paper twice, and stuffed it into his backpack. He wasn't going to tell anyone. Whoever had done this was *not* going to have the fun of seeing him be mad about it.

All morning and right up to lunch on Thursday, Clay's anger lay hidden just below the surface, and it sharpened his eyes and ears.

He kept looking at kids, watching their eyes, their smiles, their nods, the way they said hi or the way they didn't. He listened to their voices, trying to catch that mocking tone, that particular "hah, hah" of somebody in the know. Because the punk who had trashed his picture was out there, watching him, laughing at him.

At lunch Clay sat alone at a table in the far corner, his back to the wall. He had a view of the whole cafeteria, and he chewed on his chicken fingers and sipped his chocolate milk, and he watched.

Tobin spotted him and smirked, then said something to the kid sitting beside him. They both looked Clay's way and laughed.

The big, red-haired kid went on his list of suspects.

Hank caught his eye from across the cafeteria, then pointed at some girls and gave him a thumbs-up. Clay almost waved for Hank to come over. It'd be great to have some help tracking down the creep who had ruined the drawing. But he didn't want anybody feeling sorry for him, not even Hank. He just smiled back the best he could and gave Hank a nod. Then he went on with the manhunt.

James Lawler was standing in the ice-cream line. He looked around and caught Clay's eye for a second, then looked away. Clay remembered shoving James into a huge mud puddle during gym class about a month ago. Maybe the kid was still mad about that. James also had art the same period he did . . . James could have seen him putting the self-portrait into that storage cabinet. So he had a motive, plus access to the crime scene.

James went on the list.

Allie and the new girl from Florida scurried past, whispering. Then they both glanced over their shoulders at him and smirked. Clay hadn't thought about accusing any girls . . . and he didn't even know that new one yet. Was Allie mean enough to do something like this? If she was mad about something? Or if someone had dared her? Absolutely.

Allie went on the list.

Once Allie made it onto the list, it grew fast. There were so many kids who had a reason to get back at him for something—dozens and dozens. He'd been teasing and bothering and tormenting almost everyone for years.

Didn't they get that it wasn't like he was after *them*, that it wasn't personal? Because it wasn't . . . not most of the time. Most of the time, he was just having some fun.

Halfway through lunch Clay gave up on the list. He had tons of suspects, but nothing solid. And really, did he even have the right to be mad? How many times had *he* been the one secretly smiling while someone else got upset or embarrassed or laughed at?

He returned his tray and looked at the clock. Mr. Dash had told him that he always ate his lunch in the art room. So he could go there right now, start on a new self-portrait.

He turned around and headed for the doors to the playground.

He didn't want to go and have to look at himself, not right now.

Maybe later.

CHAPTER FIFTEEN

NO TRICK, NO TREAT

For the week leading up to Halloween, Mitch had been reminding Clay every day. "You know you're not goin' out to trick-or-treat with your buddies, right? It's not happening, not this year. You understand?"

And all week Clay had been nodding and saying, "Sure, I get it. No problem."

But now Halloween day had actually arrived, and it was on a Friday, too.

Across the breakfast table that morning Clay said, "How about if I just go out and trick-or-treat around our neighborhood for an hour or so tonight, just to get some candy? That'd be okay, don't you think?"

Mitch narrowed his eyes. "Sure. You can go out from five thirty to six. As long as you're back here in the house with me before dark, no problem. Knock yourself out."

Clay left for school, slamming out of the house.

Sure, he was supposed to trust *Mitch*—trust, trust, trust! But what about the flip side? When was Mitch going to start trusting *him*?

Because he was *not* going to go walk around and beg for candy when all the kindergartners were out with their mommies and daddies. Better to have no Halloween at all.

School was buzzing. There was going to be a parade in the lower grades hallway, and a lot of the little kids arrived wearing their costumes. Some of the teachers were dressed up too, even in the upper grades. Mr. Dash was wearing a huge metal helmet with horns out the sides. That, plus his red beard, made him look exactly like a Viking warrior.

Clay felt like he was watching all of it from a distance. Halloween hadn't ever felt like this before. It had always been fun—and Halloween week was the perfect time for new pranks at school. He and Hank had pulled off some good ones, too—and they'd never been caught.

There was the time in fourth grade when they glued Mrs. Moss's math book to her desk. Watching her try to pick it up? So funny!

Back in third grade they had hidden a bunch of cheap digital watches around the room. Their annoying little alarms were set to go off the day before Halloween during a state assessment test—*beep-beep-beep-beep, beep-beep-beep-beep, beep-beep-beep-beep*. Almost drove Ms. Fiori crazy. She never did find the watch behind the big metal bookcases. That thing beeped every day at 9:47 for the whole rest of that school year, plus half the next—until its battery finally died.

And just last Halloween? They had squeezed sticky ink from a ballpoint pen onto the back of the doorknob to the teachers' room, and then spent the rest of the day trying to count how many teachers had dark blue spots on their fingers: nine—ten, if you included the principal.

Clay remembered these past Halloween pranks in bits and pieces while he sat in homeroom staring out the window. He also remembered going pumpkin-smashing with Hank, and going out once with Mitch and his buddies for some late-night toilet paper attacks.

Homeroom ended, and he shuffled along with the crowd out into the hallway. A sudden thought stopped him in his tracks—he actually stood still just outside his science room: Yesterday, someone had pranked *him*—ruined his drawing! And it made him want to get back at everybody, go out and trash the whole town.

But if he did go out tonight, would he really want to do that kind of stuff? And if he *didn't*, would it even be fun to be out after dark—if there wasn't going to be any danger or adventure in it? Well, no matter what, it wasn't fair for Mitch to completely kill Halloween—Clay was sure about that.

As the day went on, he got grumpier and grouchier. He decided that his brother had turned into a royal pain in the neck. He decided that Mr. Kelling just might be a major jerk after all. He decided that getting all dressed up in costumes was definitely only for dumb little kids, and that Mr. Dash looked stupid in that giant helmet with the horns.

He didn't start on his new self-portrait during art class, and he didn't go into the art room to work on it at lunchtime, either. Why bother? And he felt like smashing all the cutesy little decorated pumpkins in the cafeteria.

He frowned his way through his afternoon classes, getting more and more annoyed at how excited all the other kids were.

A minute before the final bell, there was a loud ding, and the principal's voice came onto the PA system.

"I want to remind everyone to be extra careful if you go out trick-or-treating later on. Take a flashlight or a glow stick, and watch out whenever you cross the street. Be respectful, and don't get tricked into doing something you'll be sorry about later. I hope all of you have a safe and happy Halloween."

Just what he needed—more advice. Clay gritted his teeth and scowled all the way to his bus. As it lurched out of the driveway and rumbled toward home, he felt like he was being hauled from one prison to another one—Kelling ran his daytime jail, and Mitch was in charge everywhere else. The only thing missing was a set of handcuffs.

When they got to Tobin's stop on the ride home, the kid paused next to Clay's seat on his way along the aisle, like he was going to make a wisecrack. Then he saw the look in Clay's eyes. Tobin shut his mouth and hurried off the bus.

When he arrived home, Clay stomped into the front hall, dumped his new book bag on the floor, went straight down the back hallway into his room, and slammed the door. He threw himself onto the couch and stared up at the ceiling.

Happy Halloween.

Yeah, *right*.

CHAPTER SIXTEEN

AND A MUSTACHE

Mitchell—just leave him alone!" Mrs. Hensley stood in the doorway to the back hall. "If he wants to stay in his room, that's fine. And stop that racket—there're a bunch of little kids coming up the front walk!"

Clay hadn't come out to eat dinner, and he hadn't come out to see Anne's costume before she left with her friends for a party and a sleepover.

Mitchell had just banged on his bedroom door for the third time. He also tried to push his way into the room, but Clay had managed to block the door.

"I'm not coming out, so just go away!" That's all Clay had said, and he'd only said it once.

As it got later, the bigger kids began coming.

Mrs. Hensley was pretty sure Clay would come out when he heard some of his friends at the door. But he didn't.

A little after nine thirty, a group of older boys showed up. One of them lifted up a blood-spattered goalie mask. "Hi, Mrs. Hensley—it's me, Hank. Is Clay around?"

"He's been in his room all night. I don't think he's feeling well."

"Oh. Well, like, can I say hi to him?"

"Sure," she said.

Hank walked back to Clay's bedroom and knocked.

"Hey," he called, "yo, Clay, it's me—just wanted to say hi."

There was no answer.

Hank came back to the door and saw Mitch in the living room.

He nodded. "Hi, Mitch. So, Clay didn't go out at all?"

"Nope."

"Well, say hi for me, okay?"

"Sure."

Hank flipped his mask down, then took a few pieces of candy from the basket. He mumbled, "Thanks, Mrs. Hensley," and left.

The flow of kids coming to the door slowed to

a trickle. There was a large group of high school-ers at ten o'clock, and then it got quiet. Mitch and his mom settled in on the couch to watch *Halloween 4* and eat leftover candy.

About a half hour later, just as the faceless killer cornered a girl in a deserted drugstore, some-one knocked on the Hensleys' front door. Mrs. Hensley jumped and let out a little yelp.

Mitchell laughed, and she swatted his arm.

"It's not funny!"

She grabbed the candy basket—but it was awfully late for trick-or-treaters. She peeked through the narrow glass panel, then quickly opened the door.

Two police officers stood on the front porch, a man and a woman.

The woman tipped her cap. "Are you Mrs. Hensley?"

"Yes—did something happen?"

"Is your husband at home?"

"He's working night shift at the water plant—is he all right? Is this about him?"

"No, ma'am, it's not about him. There was an incident over on Nichols Street, and we'd like to talk to your son about it."

Mitch stepped into the front hall.

"I'm her son. I'm Mitchell Hensley."

The woman hesitated, and the man looked down at a notepad.

"We need to talk to *Clayton* Hensley," he said. "Is he here?"

"He's been in his room all night, Officer," said Mrs. Hensley.

"Do you have a warrant?" asked Mitch. "Is he being arrested?"

"No, he's not being arrested," the woman said, "not yet." She looked Mitch in the eye. "Unless you're Clayton's legal guardian, I want you to back out of this conversation that I'm having with your mother. *Are* you Clayton's legal guardian?"

Mitch shook his head.

She turned back to Mrs. Hensley. "We need to talk to Clayton. We've only got a couple questions for him."

"Mom," Mitchell said, "just shut the door. Don't say anything else. They can't come in without an invitation or a warrant, and you don't have to talk to them or answer any questions. And neither does Clay. That's the law."

The woman said, "What, you're everybody's lawyer now?"

Mrs. Hensley looked from Mitchell back to

the officer. "What—what happened on Nichols Street?"

"Eggs thrown all over a house and a car, and graffiti sprayed on the front door."

Screams and loud music came from the TV in the living room.

"Whose house was it?" asked Mrs. Hensley.

"It belongs to Alfred Kelling, the principal at your son's school." She looked at Mitch. "Your *other* son's school."

"What was on the door?" asked Mitchell.

The woman just glared at him, but the other officer spoke up.

"Looks like a donkey. With eyeglasses and a mustache."

CHAPTER SEVENTEEN

EVIDENCE

I'm going to talk to my husband, and to Clayton. Then we can talk to you. Good night, and thank you."

And with that, Mrs. Hensley closed her front door on the two police officers.

Mitch turned and walked straight into the back hallway and banged on Clay's bedroom door.

"Open up, Clay! Right now, or I swear I'm gonna get a shovel and bust my way in!"

"Clayton," his mother called, "open this door!"

There was the sound of something heavy sliding on the floor, and the door opened. Clay stood there, his shirt rumpled and his hair plastered flat against one side of his head.

"What's your problem? I told you I wasn't coming out. Leave me alone."

He flopped down onto the couch and pulled a pillow over his head.

"You been in here all night?" said Mitchell, walking over to examine the window that faced the side yard.

From under the pillow, Clay said, "Do you *trust* me, or don't you? It's a simple question."

Mitchell went to the couch and grabbed the pillow away from him. "Answer me—did you go out tonight?"

Clay sneered, "Yeah—I snuck out. And I stole a car and robbed a 7-Eleven. Then I burned down the school and toasted marshmallows over the flames. Is that what you want to hear?"

"No, but I bet the two cops who just left would love it."

Clay sat up straight. He looked at his mom. "Really? Cops?"

She nodded. "Yes. Somebody egged the principal's house."

Mitchell took a deep breath. "This is serious, Clay. They think it was you."

"Didn't you tell 'em I was here?"

"Yes, I did," said his mom, "but they wanted to talk to you anyway."

"So . . . did Mr. Kelling tell them to come here?"

"Probably," said Mitch.

"But how come?"

"Whoever threw the eggs also painted a jackass on his front door."

Mrs. Hensley gave Mitch a puzzled look. "Why would that make him think of Clayton?"

Mitch pulled out his cell phone and began punching buttons. "Clay drew a picture a couple weeks ago, and the principal saw it."

He handed her the phone, and she squinted at the small screen. Her eyebrows shot up. "Clayton, how could you!"

"It was mostly a joke, Mom. Mr. Kelling even bought the drawing off me, to keep in his office— really, he thought it was funny."

She frowned as she handed the phone back to Mitchell. "Well, if it brought two police officers to the front door on Halloween night, I wouldn't call it funny!"

"Well, anyway, I didn't do that stuff over at his house. I was here all night. That's a fact."

Mitchell shook his head. "As far as the cops are concerned, it's not a fact unless you can prove it."

"But you *know* I was here."

"Do I?" asked Mitch. "I know that you barricaded yourself into this ground-level room, and

I know this room has a low window. I know I talked to you once at quarter of six, and then now, around ten thirty. I know I didn't see you or hear you for four hours. *Those* are the facts. You *say* you were in this room that whole time. And that's what we're going to have to prove. *I* believe you, I really do. But what *you* say and what *I* believe? That still doesn't mean Kelling and the police can't build a case against you."

"So . . . what should I do?" said Clay.

Mitchell shrugged. "Wait. If they think they've got a case, the cops'll be back."

"The *first* thing you need to do," said his mom, "is have some food. You missed your dinner."

Clay smiled a little. "Yeah, that'd be good. Thanks."

While Clay was eating leftover pizza, his dad came home from work. He sat down at the kitchen table, and Mitchell explained what had been happening.

"They think Clay did it?" he said. "How come? Anybody can buy eggs."

It was Clay's turn to explain. "It's because of the picture on the door. A couple weeks ago I made a drawing, sort of a cartoon. And the principal saw it."

Mitchell punched up the image again on his phone and handed it to his dad.

Mr. Hensley took a look and laughed out loud. "Ha! You should've put this out on the Internet!"

Mrs. Hensley put her hands on her hips. "Sometimes I think you *want* these boys to end up in jail, the way you talk! It's not right to make fun of people—and sometimes it's also just plain stupid."

"The stupid part was getting caught. Come on, sweetheart, you've met that principal, and *you* don't like him any more than I do."

She shook her head. "What I'm saying is, if you're mean to other people, it comes right back at you. And that is a *mean* picture. Now finish up eating so we can get some sleep tonight. And don't give your sons any more bad advice!"

Ten minutes later Janie came home from her date, and by eleven thirty, everybody was in bed. The house got quiet.

Clay lay in the dark on the upper bunk. "Hey, Mitch, you awake?" he said softly.

"Yup."

"Like, if everything went all wrong with this stuff about the principal's house, would they take me over to the jail where you were?"

"No, there's a whole different system—there's a place just for kids over in Dixonville. You have to be at least eighteen to go into the county lockup. But don't worry about it. Nothing's gonna happen. You didn't do anything . . . right?"

"Right."

A minute later Clay said, "But let's say they find some kind of evidence, something that looks really bad, something we can't explain. If I got sent to Dixonville, would I get kicked out of school?"

"I don't know . . . probably. But like you said, you didn't do anything. They can't prove something that didn't happen, right? Listen, I've got the early shift tomorrow. Nothing's gonna happen. So go to sleep, okay?"

"Okay."

But Clay had slept on the couch most of the night. He couldn't even get his eyes to stay shut.

When he was sure Mitch was asleep, he climbed down the ladder and tiptoed across the room and out the door.

He went to the fridge to get another slice of pizza, but it was all gone.

He went into the living room and turned on the TV. It was after midnight, and there was nothing on but talk shows and a couple of horror movies. He flipped around a little, then turned it off.

He turned it right back on. Better to watch something stupid than have to sit in a completely quiet house and think. He flipped through the channels again and settled on *Abbott and Costello Meet Frankenstein*, which was more funny than scary—and that was fine with him.

The candy basket was on the low table in front of the couch, and he dug around until he found some red licorice. He peeled back the crinkly wrapping and was about to take a bite when he froze. He'd heard something.

He muted the TV, and then pulled in a sharp breath. All the hairs on his arms stood straight up. A scratching at the window, just ten feet from where he sat—then muffled laughing.

Clay exhaled—and smiled. He knew that laugh.

He jumped up and turned off the TV. He pulled the shade up halfway, unlocked the window, and pushed up the sash.

"Hey, man!" he whispered. "You 'bout scared the bedoombas outta me!"

Hank grinned up at him from the front bushes. "I was gonna knock at your bedroom window, then I peeked and saw it was you watching the tube. Want to sneak out? We've got some big plans."

The Miller brothers were in the shadows off to Hank's left. Donnie whispered, "Yeah, it's gonna be a blast!"

Clay shook his head. "Sorry, but I can't."

"*Bedawwwk—bawk-bawk-bawk . . .*" Dave started making little chicken sounds.

"Really, I can't. There were already cops here tonight. I have to stay in."

"*Cops?*" Hank whispered. "Here? You're kidding, right?"

"Not kidding," said Clay. "Somebody egged Mr. K.'s house and tagged a jackass on his door. They think it was me."

"But . . . like, weren't you home all night?"

"Yeah, but it'd be hard to prove—that's what Mitch says. 'Course, the cops have to prove stuff too. Anyway, we have to wait and see. Listen, you guys better get out of here before my folks hear you—they're probably still awake."

"Wish you could come," said Hank.

"Yeah, I wish I could too," said Clay.

"I'll call you tomorrow, okay?"

"Yeah, sure," Clay said. Then he smiled and

added, "Unless they don't let me take phone calls in jail."

Hank didn't laugh. "Later," he said.

Clay closed the window and locked it.

He stood for a minute and watched the three guys skulk away down the street. At that moment he was actually glad the police had come to his house. It had given him a good excuse for not sneaking out.

But standing there in the dark, he was honest with himself. Whether he'd had an excuse or not, he still wouldn't have gone.

CHAPTER EIGHTEEN

FUN

Clay woke up the next morning, stretched and yawned and looked at the alarm clock on the dresser. Nine thirty. He yawned again and closed his eyes. Saturday was the best.

Then he sat straight up—last night! Halloween! And cops, looking for *him*!

Clay pulled on his jeans and a T-shirt and hurried to the kitchen.

His mom was at the table with a cup of coffee and the paper. She smiled at him.

"I'm glad you had a good rest—how late did you and Mitch stay up?"

"Not late at all. Heard from the police yet?"

She shook her head. "Nope. And that's just fine. Except, if they do mean to come after you,

I'd like to know right away, rather than keep wondering."

"Yeah, me too," he said.

"You want eggs and bacon?"

"No thanks—I'm just gonna have some toast and then mow the lawn." This far into the fall the grass wasn't growing much, but mowing was a paying job, and Clay wanted to do the work no matter what. Besides, the leaves had begun to fall, and he liked mowing a whole lot better than raking.

After breakfast he went to the garage and rolled the old power mower out onto the driveway. He checked the oil and the gas, then yanked on the starter cord. It finally started after about ten pulls, and he turned around and pushed it toward the front lawn. That's when he noticed the street—at least a dozen smashed pumpkins, all the way up and down Monroe Street.

Hank and Dave and Donnie had done this, almost for sure. He started to laugh, then stopped himself. A month ago he'd have seen something like this, and he would have grinned and whispered, "Awesome!"

He remembered last Halloween. He'd slept over at Hank's, and around one in the morning

they snuck out and went smashing—you grab a pumpkin, run out into the street and whip it way up in the air, and then wait for that *thwomp* when it hits the concrete and explodes. Then run to the next house, the next pumpkins. And when that guy came out in his pajamas and started chasing them? It had been a wild night, so much fun!

Back then.

But this morning, in the light of day? Clay looked up and down the block, and all he saw was a big mess. And he imagined the little kids who had carved their own jack-o'-lanterns, looking at the broken chunks out in the street.

He shrugged and started mowing. He pushed the noisy machine back and forth, back and forth, and he wondered if anything was ever going to feel like fun again.

He knew what Hank thought about him—that he was afraid to goof around now, afraid of the rules, afraid to have any fun at all.

Fun—there was that word again. What did it mean, anyway?

Was it fun to mow the lawn? No. Not fun.

But . . . it did feel good when he was done. And when his dad looked the job over and said, "Nice work," that felt good too. And getting paid his allowance money? That absolutely *was* fun.

Was it fun to be doing better in his classes now? Fun wasn't the right word, because it was hard work—a lot harder than mowing a lawn.

But in math last Wednesday, when the teacher handed back the big test on binomials? Like always, Mr. Brighton wrote the name of every kid who got 90 percent or better up on the board. And *his* name was up there for the first time— Clay Hensley.

Was that fun? Yeah . . . kind of. And when some of the other kids whose names were up on the board all the time turned and stared at him? Seeing the looks on their faces? That was kind of fun too.

When he was done mowing and sweeping up, his dad came outside to look things over.

"That's a good job." He pulled some bills out of his pocket and peeled off a ten and a five. "Don't throw this away buying junk food—unless you share it with me."

He said that every week, and every week they both laughed. His dad started to go back inside, then stopped and looked at Clay.

"Listen, what your mom was saying last night? She's right. That picture you drew was a pretty cheap shot, and it wasn't smart, either. And if you'd stuck it out on the Web or somewhere, you'd probably be in even bigger trouble. No more cheap shots, you hear me?"

"Yes, sir."

His dad sat down heavily on the front steps. "I don't know what'll happen with you and the cops. And it tears me up inside how I can't help out, not one bit. And Mitch was in jail for a whole month. Any of you kids gets in trouble with the law, all I can do is watch. Tears me up. I don't know if I can stand another son being in trouble that way. I just hope it all comes to nothing."

Clay nodded, then mumbled, "Me too."

He didn't know what else to say. His dad hadn't talked to him like this before.

"Guess I'll put the mower away."

His dad stood up. "Yup. And be sure you clean that air filter, okay?"

"I always do."

Clay wheeled the mower into the garage. He unscrewed the filter cover and turned on the air compressor. He took the filter unit apart and used the blow gun to blast the grit and grass and leaves off the thick white paper. Then he shut off the compressor and reassembled the filter. All the while, he kept thinking about what his dad had said.

So . . . he'd been really upset about Mitchell being in jail? That made sense, of course, but it hadn't even occurred to Clay when it was happening. Mostly because his dad was always so gruff and full of fight. He had yelled about how unfair the judge was, and he had snarled about lawyers and cops and radar traps and speed limit signs. His dad grumbled and groused about almost everything. But under all of that, he was—what had he said?—all torn up. Inside.

Clay pushed the mower back to its spot, and then stood still, looking down the driveway at the street. And the pumpkins.

And he imagined his dad feeling all torn up about *him*.

It wasn't fun.

CHAPTER NINETEEN

ALMOST FREE

"Hey, Mom?" Clay was out on the driveway, straddling his bicycle. "I'm gonna ride over to the comics store, okay?"

She came to the screen door. "I don't think that's a good idea, Clay. Mitchell can drive you there when he gets home from work."

"Look, I'm gonna ride to ComiKazee, buy one comic book with my own money, and then ride straight back—a half hour, tops. And if Mitchell gets home before I do, you can tell him I'm wearing my helmet and obeying all the bike safety laws. And you can also tell him that he's not my boss."

"I really don't think you . . ."

That was all Clay heard her say. He was down the driveway and gone, pedaling hard, the wind fluttering in his ears. He didn't really want a new comic book, but he *did* want to get away from everybody for a while.

He went up Monroe Street two blocks, took a right on Ewing, and when he got to Tenth Street, he went left. He was careful to signal all his turns.

The comic book shop was only about six blocks ahead on Bluff Street, just a little south of Tenth. The air whipping past him was crisp and cool, the November sky was blue, and the sun warmed his face. He hadn't felt so free and happy in weeks.

A few intersections later he glanced up at the street sign, and then slammed on his brakes and planted both feet on the pavement.

It was Nichols Street. That was the street where Mr. K. lived.

Maybe . . . nah—he didn't even know the guy's address.

But how tough could it be to spot his house? It was the one with a jackass spray-painted on the front door. And he really wanted to get a look at it.

Clay took off his helmet, then pulled up the hood of his sweatshirt. He opened the headband inside the helmet as far as it would go, then pulled it back on over the hoodie. It probably looked strange that way, but having the hood up would keep his face a little more hidden. He pushed off and swung his handlebars to the right. He felt like a spy heading into enemy territory.

Nichols Street sloped slightly downhill, and with a little effort he could have zoomed. Instead, he kept touching his brakes. He cruised along slowly, scanning the homes on both sides of the street. The houses here looked pretty much like his—most of them ranch-style, most about the same size, most of them with one-car garages.

It was a long way between cross streets, and after the first four blocks, he started wondering if he had recalled the name of Mr. K.'s street correctly. After six blocks, he started thinking he should just turn around and go to the comics store. All he was seeing on front doors were bundles of Indian corn, or Halloween decorations like paper skeletons and black cats.

There weren't many people outside either—a few neat freaks trying to rake up every single leaf, a white-haired lady on a ladder cleaning the gutters of her garage, and a man riding a big tractor mower on a small front lawn.

As he crossed Third Street, up ahead he saw a guy in a ripped sweatshirt picking up broken pumpkin pieces from his front walk. Would Hank and the Miller brothers have come this far south? No—must have been done by someone else who liked the sound of smashing pumpkins. Still scanning side to side, he didn't see an egged house or car, and no spray-painted front door.

As he glided past the man cleaning up the pumpkin, Clay noticed the logo on his sweatshirt—it was an old Cardinals baseball hoodie, the same as his. He grinned, and was ready to yell out "Go Cardinals!" to the guy, but he saw his face. It was Mr. Kelling.

Clay quickly turned his head to the side and pedaled like mad, pouring on speed. After half a block he slowed down, checked for traffic, and then wheeled around, facing the other way. He came to a stop, his right foot resting on the curb.

He looked back up the block, and he could see Mr. K. He was on his porch now, a small bucket in one hand and a brush in the other. He was painting his front door.

Clay's first thought was to get away from there, fast.

But . . . why? Hadn't he been face-to-face with Mr. K. dozens of times before—in situations when they had both known he was completely guilty?

This was different. This time, more than anything,

Clay wanted to make Mr. K. see he was innocent.

He pedaled slowly back up the block. His heart began thumping in his chest. He wasn't sure if this was going to be the bravest thing he'd ever done, or the dumbest thing.

Either way, he was going to do it. He had to.

CHAPTER TWENTY

SCENE OF THE CRIME

C lay rode up onto the sidewalk in front of Mr. Kelling's house. His driveway was still wet, and the garden hose and a bucket were next to a gray minivan. Bits of white eggshell had washed down onto the sidewalk.

He steered around some pumpkin slime, hung a right turn, and rolled up the principal's front walk. Fifteen feet ahead, Mr. K. was putting a second coat of white paint on his front door.

Clay could still see the outlines of the jackass. It had been made with red spray paint, except for the glasses and the mustache, which must have been black. It was going to take at least three coats of white paint to fully cover it.

When he stopped, his front brakes made a little

squeak. The principal didn't turn around, didn't stop painting.

Before Clay could speak, Mr. Kelling said, "I thought that was you riding by, Clayton. And when you sped up, I was almost certain."

He still had his back to Clay. After a few more strokes, he laid his brush across the top of the paint bucket and turned around. He looked down from the porch, no warmth in his eyes. When he spoke, his voice had an icy edge.

"So, are you returning to the scene of the crime? They say a guilty person can't resist doing that."

At school, when the principal was angry, it had always seemed funny to Clay, always made him feel like laughing in the guy's face. Right now the man was a hundred times scarier than he had ever been at school.

Clay gulped, and his first few words came out high and squeaky.

"I . . . I got scared when I saw you, but I came back. And I came back because I wanted to tell you myself that I didn't do this. I didn't—"

The principal held up his hand. "You *say* you didn't do this, but it certainly seems possible, even probable." He nodded at the door. "That is a very distinctive image—*your* image."

"Well, yeah . . . ," said Clay, "but whoever painted it there wasn't any good at drawing. And anyway, I didn't even leave my house last night. I mean . . . if I hadn't ever made that picture, no one would have tried to copy it onto your door. So I'm sorry about that. But I still didn't do *this*. And I wouldn't have. I—I just wouldn't have done this. Or thrown the eggs, either. Last year, or even back in September, I might have. But not since the last few weeks. And that's the truth."

Mr. Kelling's eyes narrowed. "How do you even *know* about this, and about the eggs? Because if you *didn't* do it, then you must have heard about it from whoever *did*."

Clay shook his head. "The police came to my house last night and talked to my mom and my brother. They told us what happened. And they came because you must have told them that you thought it was me."

Mr. Kelling nodded. "When they asked if I had any idea who might have done it, I thought of you, first thing. And I told them so."

A question formed in Clay's mind, and he frowned. "But . . . when we talked in your office after I threw that cheese in the cafeteria? I said I wasn't going to do stuff like that anymore. And you said you were going to take me at my word, remember?"

"Of course I do."

"So then, last night . . . you decided I had broken my word, right?"

"I—I was very angry. And looking at the evidence, it did seem like something you might have done. After all, you and I have a long history together, Clayton. It's only been very recently that our . . . our communication has begun to improve."

The principal paused, his mustache twitching a little. "Tell me this," he said. "How many people do you think saw that drawing you made, besides you and me?"

Clay thought a second. "Everybody in my art class saw it, plus Hank Bowers and some other kids out in the hallway. And my brother and my mom and dad. And I bet a ton of the kids in art class described the drawing to their friends. So that's a lot of people. And Mrs. Ormin saw it too."

"Well," the principal said, "I think we can be pretty certain that Mrs. Ormin didn't do this."

They both smiled at that idea.

Mr. Kelling walked down the steps. Standing level with Clay, he wasn't all that much taller.

He looked at him and said, "I believe that you've been keeping your word to me. I doubted that last night, but right now I'm sure I was wrong. And I'm going to call the police and tell them you are not a suspect."

He held out his right hand, and Clay reached over and shook it, looking him square in the eye.

"And Clayton, I want to thank you for having the courage to come and talk to me about this. And I'm sorry that my suspicions brought the police to your home. That must have upset your parents—and your brother, too."

Clay nodded. "Yeah, I don't think my mom and dad got much sleep last night."

"I didn't sleep well either. How about you?" the principal asked.

"Me?" Clay smiled. "I knew I hadn't done anything wrong. I slept fine."

CHAPTER TWENTY-ONE

BATTLE TO THE END

Second period was half over. It was a rainy Monday morning, which meant indoor gym class. The final activity was dodgeball. After a furious ten minutes, Clay was the last player for the red team, and Hank was the only survivor from the blue team.

Hank circled right, and Clay quickly backed away to the left—he had great respect for his friend's wicked right arm.

Three minutes earlier, everyone except Hank had been knocked off the blue team—leaving him alone to face six red players. With a ball in each hand, Hank deflected the body shots. He jumped the leg shots, dodging and twirling away from every assault. And lashing out with that right arm of his, he had picked off the red shooters like a one-man SWAT team.

Now it was just Hank and Clay, locked in a battle to the end.

Clay took a run at the line, acting like he was coming in for a strike. Hank took the bait and threw, but his shot was a little high. Clay felt the blast of air as the ball almost grazed his head.

"Hey, no head shots!" yelled Mr. Garland. "I want to see good sportsmanship out there!"

Hank dashed to grab another ball, and when he bent down, Clay let loose. His throw was right on target, but Hank dropped to the floor and the ball bounced foul.

Hank charged the line, expecting Clay to back up, but he didn't. From only fifteen feet apart they each whipped a shot. The balls collided, and then bounced wide and rolled out of play. Clay ran back to get another ball—and there weren't any.

"Lookin' for one of these?" Hank called.

He walked casually toward the center line with one ball under his left arm while dribbling a second one like a basketball. "Hold nice and still, and I won't hurt you."

Clay grinned and lifted both his arms out wide. With a quick windup, Hank blasted a rocket right at his knees. Clay jumped sideways, but he kept his eyes on that second ball. Even though he saw it coming, there was nothing he could do. It was Hank's deadly sidearm throw, roaring in chest-high and timed perfectly—he was completely off balance. The ball hit his left shoulder with so much force that Clay was knocked back onto his rear end.

But that same force also sent the red ball twenty-five feet straight up into the air. Still sitting on the floor, Clay looked up, locked in on the ball, scooched backward, put up his hands, and caught it.

Both teams burst into wild cheering, and Mr. Garland blew his whistle and shouted, "Red team wins! Great game, everybody, great game! Okay, class is over in five minutes, so let's get this place cleaned up."

Hank came over and offered Clay a hand, then pulled him up off the floor.

"That was a lucky catch, Hensley," he said.

"Yeah," said Clay, "losers always say stuff like that."

Hank grinned and gave him a punch on the shoulder.

"Hey," Clay said, using Mr. Garland's tone of voice, "sportsmanship, sportsmanship!"

There were plenty of kids gathering up the cones and the balls, so Clay and Hank turned in their colored vests, then walked to the bleachers and got their backpacks. They sat on a stack of blue and yellow mats to wait for the bell.

"Seriously, you *killed* out there today," Clay said, "like, *Medal of Honor* deadly—really."

Hank smiled. "You were decent too." He cleared his throat, paused, then cleared it again. "Sorry I didn't call you, you know, after Halloween night. You hear anything else from the cops?"

Clay shook his head. "Nope. It's all over."

"Seriously?"

"Yeah," said Clay. "I rode my bike over to Mr. K.'s house Saturday."

"No way! What happened?"

Clay shrugged. "Not much. I told him I didn't do it, and he believed me. Then he called the cops and told them to back off. End of story."

"That's great," said Hank.

"Yeah, I'm glad it's settled."

Hank bounced his heels against the mats six or seven times, then stopped. He took a deep breath and started talking, low and fast.

"Listen, Clay, I'm the one who did that stuff at Kelling's house. Dave and Donnie were there too, but it was my idea. But I wasn't trying to get you in trouble or anything, I really wasn't. It was just . . . like, goofing around. And painting the picture on the door? I was just trying to be funny. If I'd thought they'd come looking for you, I never would've done it. I really wouldn't have."

Clay was quiet a moment. Then he said, "Don't worry about it. I know you wouldn't have tried to get me in trouble." He paused, then added, "And really, I kind of figured out it might have been you who did it."

Hank turned and looked at him. "Yeah? How come?"

Clay grinned. "Because it was the kind of thing I might have done, and you're the only other kid I know who's as crazy as I am."

Hank laughed, but then he added, "You mean, as crazy as you *used* to be, right?" His face darkened, and he looked at the floor. "I loved whipping all those eggs, and if I could have nailed Mr. K. himself, that would've felt even better. I don't know how that guy got to you, but he did, right? Kelling really got to you. Changed everything."

"What? No," said Clay. "That's not it. It was

Mitch. He got out of jail and he came back home all freaked out, said I had to stop getting in so much trouble. He's the one who made me get my hair cut and—"

"Mitch? He was in *jail*?" Hank stared at him. "You never told me that."

Clay shrugged. "Yeah, well, my mom said not to talk about it. But I thought everybody knew. It was in the paper."

Hank said, "So, not messing around anymore after school . . ."

"Mitch."

"Or hanging out on Halloween . . ."

"Mitch," Clay said again. "And doing all my homework, and dressing like a dork, it was all Mitch's idea."

"Okay . . . ," Hank said slowly, "but it's been a pretty long time now. And it's not like Mitch is holding your hand and forcing you to be Mr. Goody-Goody every second of every day. So . . . it's partly *you* being like that. Right?"

"Yeah, I guess so," said Clay. "It's partly me. I mean, a guy can still have a little fun without being a total goof-off, right?"

"If you say so."

"I *know* so," said Clay.

Hank rolled his eyes. "Oh, so now you're the big know-it-all, too—you've got everything all figured out, right?"

"No," Clay said, "not everything. Like, 'Can you and me still hang out together?' I don't know the answer to *that* one yet."

"So . . . ," said Hank, "who gets to decide about that? Mitch?"

Clay laughed. "Don't play dumb with me, Bowers. You know who gets to decide."

Hank smiled, then raised one eyebrow. "So . . . do you want to meet up at lunch today?"

The bell rang, and they both stood up.

"Well, actually—," Clay began, but Hank interrupted him.

"Oh—right, that art thing you're doing." Then he smiled. "Hey—I'm glad I remembered. Check this out."

Hank reached into the pocket of his hoodie and then handed Clay two expensive drawing pencils. "I found these at my house. They're my sister's, but she said I could give 'em to you, if you want them. To help with your project."

Clay looked at the pencils, and then at Hank. There was an odd look on Hank's face, just for half a second.

Instantly, Clay knew. He knew why Hank was doing this. It was to make up for something *else* he had done. In the art room. When he trashed that self-portrait.

Clay clenched his jaw muscles. The blinding red anger flashed through his head, screaming, "*Payback!*" In two seconds he could snap both of those fancy pencils in half and then punch Hank in the stomach and knock him down and shout at him and tell him what a rotten friend he was.

Clay didn't do that.

He kept looking at Hank's face, and he breathed. Then he smiled.

"Really?" he said. "I can have these? They're tons better than the ones I've got now. This is great—thanks."

"No problem," said Hank.

"Listen," Clay said, "I think I'll skip the art thing at lunch. So, yeah, let's hang out."

Hank grinned at him. "Great," he said. "Meet you after chorus, okay? And maybe we'll play a little dodgeball outside after lunch. Sound like fun?"

"Definitely," said Clay. "Sounds good."

EPILOGUE

S hortly after Thanksgiving, Mrs. Ormin noticed that the students who were sent to the principal's office for discipline seemed less frightened of Mr. Kelling—no one was bursting into tears anymore. She knew why. That drawing Clayton had made? The principal had gotten it framed, and it sat on the filing cabinet right behind his desk. Someone who was able to laugh at himself just wasn't that scary.

True to his word, Clay wasn't sent to the office again for the whole rest of sixth grade. Mrs. Ormin was happy for him, but she missed his regular visits, and she also missed making the regular additions to his student folder—her masterpiece. She felt like her shorthand skills were beginning to get a little rusty.

On the next-to-last day of school, Mrs. Ormin began double-checking the records of the departing sixth graders. After adding the final grade report, she placed each student folder into a large cardboard file box—she would fill three of them by the time she was done. The school district's delivery van probably wouldn't haul the boxes of records over to the junior high until August, but Mrs. Ormin believed in doing things sooner rather than later.

The phones were quiet, and the building was almost empty—the kids and teachers were outside for the big field day. She made great progress with her task during the morning. When Mr. Kelling came in to check his messages at lunchtime, she had only one question for him.

"Mr. Kelling, would you take a look at this folder for me? I just want to be sure that everything's in order."

The principal adjusted his glasses and flipped through the pages. "Let's see—health forms, emergency contact information, testing records, residency, birth certificate, grade reports—this all seems fine to me. Do you see a problem?"

"No, sir, I don't. I just wanted to be sure I had it right. Now then, you have three messages . . .

and this is the one you should probably deal with before lunch."

Mr. Kelling went into his office and closed the door, and Mrs. Ormin went back to her filing. But she had some trouble. Her eyes were watering. Actually, she had to blink back a few tears. She smiled and thought, Who would have ever thought that the principal could make *me* cry?

Somehow, Clayton Hensley's folder had shrunk. Dozens and dozens of notes and transcripts and complaints and referral forms—six and a half years of trouble—had vanished from his permanent student folder. He would be starting junior high with a clean record.

Beyond the basic information, only one sheet of paper had been added to Clayton's folder, a pale green page from the school's December newsletter. A paragraph had been circled:

Truman Student Is Honored

It's a pleasure to announce that sixth grader Clay Hensley recently earned an honorable mention in a countywide art contest. More than two hundred students in grades five through eight submitted self-portraits for this competition. One grand prize was awarded, and three honorable mentions. We are all very proud of Clay, and here is what the contest judges had to say:

> In addition to his fine photo-realistic pencil work, Clayton Hensley has added humor and intensity by including two faces in this remarkable self-portrait. The half-removed mask he is holding is especially interesting. It is clearly the same boy, but with the addition of the long nose and ears of a donkey.

Andrew Clements is the author of more than sixty books for children, including the enormously popular *Frindle*; the *New York Times* bestsellers *No Talking* and *Lunch Money*, and the Benjamin Pratt & the Keepers of the School series. He lives with his wife in central Massachusetts, and has four grown children.